Samuel Eason

The Guiding Star

Samuel Eason

The Guiding Star

ISBN/EAN: 9783337410162

Printed in Europe, USA, Canada, Australia, Japan

Cover: Foto ©Andreas Hilbeck / pixelio.de

More available books at **www.hansebooks.com**

THE

GUIDING STAR,

—FOR—

THE USE OF ALL PERSONS

—AS—

Their Guide Through Life

BY SAMUEL EASON.

SPRINGFIELD, OHIO
1883.

CONTENTS.

THE GUIDING STAR.

MORAL EDUCATION.

NE of the greatest of American preachers once said:
"By education, men mean almost exclusively intellectual training. For this, schools and colleges are
instituted, and to this the moral and religious discipline of the young is sacrificed. Now I reverence, as much
as any man, the intellect; but let me never exalt it above
the moral principle. With this it is most intimately connected. In this its culture is founded; and to exalt this is
its highest aim. Whoever desires that his intellect may
grow up to soundness, to healthy vigor, must begin with
moral discipline."

In the above quotation, our sentiment is expressed precisely. What is said by this distinguished divine has long
been held by us. We would not for one moment underate,
or speak disparagingly of, intellectual education. We prize
it highly; and claim that only those who love it, and attain
unto it to some considerable extent, are on the road to success in life. But we hold that morality is highly essential
to the man seeking knowledge in general. Morality is the
foundation stone. All great men have attributed their success in life more to the moral habits acquired in life than to
anything else.

"When a man looks into himself, he discovers two distinct orders or kinds of principles, which it behooves him especially to comprehend. He discovers desires, appetites, passions, which terminate in himself, which crave and seek his own interest, gratification, and distinction. And he discovers another principle, an antagonist to these, which is impartial, disinterested, universal, enjoining on him a regard to the rights and happiness of other beings, and laying on him obligations which *must* be discharged, cost what they may, or however they may clash with his particular pleasure or gain. No man, however narrowed to his own interest, however hardened by selfishness, can deny that there springs up within him a great idea in opposition to interest, the idea of duty, that an inward voice calls him, more or less distinctly, to revere and exercise impartial justice and universal good will. This disinterested principle in human nature we call sometimes reason, sometimes conscience, sometimes the *moral sense* or faculty. But, be its name what it may, it is a real principle in each of us, and it is the supreme power within us, *to be cultivated above all others*, for on its culture the right development of all others depend."

How important it is for parents to impress this grand truth upon the hearts of their children to-day. Many children, even when they have arrived to the age of mature judgment, do not seem to understand that in childhood they are molding characters, which are to shape their lives, and largely determine their future. The duty of their guardians, then, is to make a strong effort to make them see this. "That childhood is the proper period for education," says one, "is one of the most obvious of all general truths. The law on which it is founded holds good in all countries, and all times. Its range is not limited to human kind. It traverses the boundaries of the animal kingdom, and determines the form of a branch as well as the character of a man. The world teems with analogies, both real and obvious, whereby the moralist may enforce the duty of educating in the comparatively pliable period of youth. You may, within certain limits, determine at will the direction of a river, a tree, a man, if you touch them near their sources, where they are tiny and tender; but none of these, when full grown, can be bent, except in very minute degrees, and at an expense of labor greatly disproportionate to the result."

I must confess, I am passionately fond of children—good children. In the street, in the Sunday school, on the playground—*wherever* I fall in with these dear little creatures, I can not but love them, and think of the great possibilities which lie in their pathway.

They are the hope of the nation How grand, noble, and influential may their lives become! If trained well morally and intellectually, nothing can possibly hinder them from becoming noble men and women. Why just think; out of that dingy dirty faced group of boys playing yonder, are probably to come the doctors, ministers, and lawyers of the future.

And yet, on the other hand, these same boys, now so cheerful, now so bright in their play, may grow up in ignorance, and become a set of thieves, drunkards, or even murderers. What a grave responsibility, therefore, rests upon the parents of these little ones. I frequently wonder if they consider, as they ought, what is entrusted to their charge. It is said "as the twig is bent so the tree is inclined." How true! As with trees, so with children. The mother and father of these children are rapidly passing away. Soon they will be gone. Their children are largely to fill their places; and how can they do so creditably and satisfactorily

unless they are trained well *morally*, intellectually, and religiously ?

Moral education should be enforced for several reasons.
*First, because such education is necessary in order to be truly
successful in life..*   This truth needs little to verify itself.
Every day and in all the walks of life, we see evidence manifold to prove the very great value of a good moral education.
Our business men to-day seek for their help those men and
those only whom they believe have had a tolerably good
moral training.   They, and all others who try to succeed in
their business, avoid those who show the least sign of a de-
fective education morally.   And in this they are right.   No
man wants in his employ a dishonest person—one who is
always seeking an opportunity to shove a cent down into his
own pocket.   What the universal world needs to-day above
all else is honest, straightforward, christian men—men who
act from principle, and who do right because it is right.

" There are men who choose honesty as a soul companion.   They live in it, and with it, and by it.   They embody
it in their actions and lives.   Their words speak it.   Their
faces beam it.   Their actions proclaim it.   Their hands are
true to it.   They love it.   It is to them like a God.   They
believe it is of God.   With religious awe they obey its be-
hests.   Not gold, or crowns, or fame, could bribe them to
leave it.   They are wedded to it from choice.   It is their
first love.   It makes them beautiful men ; yea, more, noble
men, great, brave, righteous men.   When He looks about
for His jewels, these are the men His eye rests upon, well
pleased.   He keeps his angels employed in making crowns
for them, and they make crowns for themselves, too.
Crowns of honesty !   To some men they seem not very
beautiful in the dim light of earth ; but when the radiance
of heaven is opened upon them, they will reflect it in gor-

geous splendor. · Nothing is brighter ; nothing is better ; nothing is worth more, or more substantial. Honesty, peerless queen of principles! How her smile enhaloes the men who love her! How ready they are to suffer for her, to die for her. They are the martyrs. See them. What a multitude! Some at the stake, some in stocks, some in prison ; some before judges as criminals, some on gibbets, and some on the cross. They have peace within. They are strong and brave in heart. Their souls are dauntless as the bright, old sun."

Second. Such an education in morality is necessary in order to wear well in society.

It will be admitted by every fair minded and rational being, that no man who is without good morals can be welcomed and entertained in good society. As the business man shuns the dishonest and immoral man, so does society. An immoral man, a man who has never been properly trained in morality, is a dangerous element in any society or community. Without such training he "is under *eternal quarentine* ; no friend to greet ; no home to harbor him. The voyage of his life becomes a joyless peril ; and in the midst of all ambition can achieve, or avarice amass, or rapacity plunder, he tosses on the surge, a *buoyant pestilence.*"

It is a trite, but true maxim, that "a man is known by the company he keeps." If a man is a good, moral, upright man, he will associate with such men. If he is a bad man, he will not content himself in the company of good men. He will seek his own, and there will he remain. "Better be alone than in bad company." "Evil communications corrupt good manners." "All qualities are catching as well as diseases ; and the mind is at least as much, if not a great deal more, liable to infection.than the body. Go with mean people, and you think life is mean."

Let then, these great truths be impressed upon the minds of the young by their parents. Teach them the importance of being well trained morally. Talk to them plainly con-cerning these things, so that when they arrive at the age of maturity, they may see for themselves the infinite value of morality. Parents, see to it that your children have the proper training. Keep them always in the best company, and they will hardly go wrong. The sad consequences of evil associations is exhibited in the history of almost all criminals. The case of a man, recently hanged in Canada, is an example. On the gallows, he made the following speech to those in attendance : "This is a solemn day for me, boys. I hope this will be a warning to you against bad company. I hope it will be a lesson to all young people, and old as well as young, rich and poor. It was that that brought me here to-day to my last end, though I am inno-cent of the murder I am about to suffer for. Before my God I am innocent of the murder ! I never committed this or any other murder. I am going to meet my maker in a few minutes. May the Lord have mercy on my soul. Amen, amen." What a terrible warning is this to the young. Let them never deviate from the right. Let par-ents and guardians instruct them well in morality. Let them see that their children are trained in the way they should go, knowing and believing that when they become old they will not depart from it.

RELIGIOUS EDUCATION.

E should be educated religiously. Wedo not mean by this that it is possible for a person to be so trained, so educated in religious and holy subjects, doctrines, &c., as that his knowledge in these things shall save him. Not at all. We believe emphatically in the truth uttered by our Lord while here in the flesh that "ye *must* be born again." All knowledge is to be encouraged and cultivated that man may rise to his true dignity; but "to pursue other branches to the neglect of the only two which are of universal importance—the knowledge of God, and of our own soul—is surely to be wisely, foolish and ignorantly learned. There are homes where religion is ignored. There is no worship of God there, neither is there any right religious training of the young. God is practically dethroned, and it is possible that what is called education may be completed, and yet no religion taught. Nay, men professing to be wise, have risen up to argue that religion should not be taught at all—it should be left, they say, to the unbiassed mind of youth to select the form or the creed which seems best, when entering upon life. Some of these men are called philosophers, not a few of them hold the rank of lawgivers, and their plan is practically this: 'Educate for earth, let heaven alone; educate for man, leave God out of view; educate for time, eternity will be considered anon.'"

No, this is a wrong idea. This is a mistake. It will never do to be so very particular about making preparation for their life, and do nothing to insure happiness in the next.

We are bidden in the sacred word of truth to train up our children in the way they should go, and when they become old they will not depart from it. But how few do this! They (the children) have only a partial training—a training that fits them for the duties and pleasures of earth alone. "Creation is studied, the Creator is neglected. Laws are examined, the Law-giver is unheeded. Even parents connive at and encourage such views, and since they choose to train their children in ignorance of a Father who is in Heaven, or of the worship which is his due, would it be wonderful though such children grew up despising the parents who had trained them so? If more pains be taken to teach our children the length of a Greek syllable, some one has said, than the knowledge of God, and of themselves, what wonder though ungodliness prevail? What would be the effect were the sun swept from his place among the stars? Chaos to our globe once more, and, in like manner, when religion is omitted in training a moral being, a moral chaos must ensue." The home is the place for the religious training of children. If "the church is a family," it is conversely true that a family should be a church. The well-being and future happiness of every household depends very largely upon the proper religious training of the young. Some one has wisely said, "Heaven is nearer to us in infancy than ever after."

If this be so, the utmost care should be taken in the training of infant minds while thus young, while their minds and hearts are so susceptible to religious truth.

Several reasons may here be given to show why children should have early religious training.

First. That they may understand and know the great end of life.

Many there are in this world who have yet to learn that the aim of their lives should be to glorify God, their Maker. Pleasures, wealth, honor, and happiness should not be made, as they frequently are, the chief objects of life. We were made to honor and glorify our Maker, and unless the children are early trained religiously, they are very apt to grow up in life with but very little desire to inquire after and please God. "Wisdom and affection combine to teach us that in youth—in youth above all other periods—should truth be lodged in the mind, and tended there by the hand of parental wisdom — like southern exotics from northern skies. Even then, no doubt, truth may make no more impression on the mind than an image produces on the mirror which reflects it; yet, while parents act in faith and hope, it would be at once unwise and cruel to withhold that mightiest of all influences, the truth, which the Spirit blesses to mold the soul, or give happiness instead of misery, and life instead of death.

Scripture is so full of the home feeling, or family religion, that we violate all its teaching if the love of God be not paramount, and the fear of the Lord the beginning of wisdom to our children. The christian mother especially can deeply plant and genially cherish the seeds of truth. Is her child sick? That is a text from which to speak of the Great Physician. Is it the sober calm of evening, when even children grow sedate? She can tell of the home where there is no night. It is morning when all are buoyantly happy? The eternal day is suggested, and its glories may be told. That is the wisdom which wins souls even more than the formal lesson, the lecture or the task."

Second. Children should receive an early religious training in order that they may walk into the same religious path, and grow up in the same church of their parents.

This is a very important matter, and parents know it, and believe it. Nothing preys upon the minds of parents more than this subject. They desire above all else that their children grow up in the church of which they are members, and that those children perform the duties which they duinrg life time, were permitted only to execute in part. Their mantle they wish to fall upon their children.

How few seem to think upon this subject as they should! If more attention were given it on the part of parents and guardians, a vast amount of good would be done in the world, an incalculable influence for good would be exerted upon men even after many who are now entrusted with the training of youth have fallen into the tomb. It requires no effort on the part of the dullest person living to see that this is so, for it is manifest that, provided the children are prop- erly taught in the church and religion of their parents, that they will grow up in said church, and faith to carry forward the works which their fathers were allowed to commence but not spared to finish.

"Science has sometimes tried to teach us that if a pebble be cast into the sea on any shore, the effects are felt, though not perceived by man, over the whole area of the ocean. Or, more wonderful still, science has tried to show that the effects of all the sounds ever uttered by man or beast, or caused by inanimate things, are still floating in the air ; its present state is just the aggregate result of all these sounds ; and if these things be true they furnish an emblem of the effects produced by a mother's power,—effects which stretch into eternity, and operate there forever, in sorrow or in joy. The mother is the angel—spirit of home.

Her tender yearnings over the cradle of her infant babe,

her guardian care of the child and youth, and her bosom companionship with the man of her love and choice, make her the personal center of the interests, the hopes and the happiness of the family. Her love glows in her sympathies, and reigns in all her thoughts and deeds. It never cools, never tires, never dreads, never sleeps, but ever glows and burns with increasing ardor, and with sweet and holy incense upon the altar of home devotion. Such is the influence of a parent, a mother ; such the influence that may be exerted by those wishing and striving to give their offspring a moral and religious education."

STRENGTH IN FELLOWSHIP.

THE world in all its myriad employments and affairs, wants strength. Strong individuals are always at a premium. Strength is recognized as a prime quality in manhood and womanhood. A sound mind in a sound body has ever stood as the human ideal. But there can be no truly sound mind, in God's test of soundness, that has not Christ in it. This is a vital fact. Christ is for the Christian the source of all true strength and soundness. This strength is not found in self-conceit, but in self-consecration ; not in self-seeking, but in self-surrender. For the Christian to be strong is not to be self-centered, but Christ-centered. When the highest human love and longing lay hold on the divine sympathy and help, the result is strength of character, of purpose, and of will; and this kind of Christians it is that the world sorely needs—Christians strong in faith, in hope, in humility, in patience, in love, in gentleness, in service—Christians who commend Christianity eveywhere by their practical living of it.

The place where this Christian strength is fostered and made felt is in the church of Christ. The old question is ever to be met, "Can not I be a Christian and live a Christian life without joining the church?" Perhaps, in God's grace, you can, but the chances are all against you, and you can not be an obedient follower and do it. On the other hand the church is the Christian league. Its members are banded together, for what? To insure greater strength for service, more perfect protection against the common enemy, sin, and enlarged efficiency in the winning of souls. Pre-eminently the purpose is to be mutually helpful, to realize in practice the divine command, "Bear ye one another's burdens." To share in sympathy and love, which is to help bear; to strengthen each where each is weak, and thus all become stronger together and thus to seek to bring those who are outside within this mutually helpful circle— this is what the church is for. And the church is strong and helpful above every other organization, because in it not only is each true member bound to every other, but each is bound to the great Head of the church, Christ.

This being true, then, that the church is God's chosen means to strengthen his people individually, and God's chosen instrument through which to extend the saving knowledge of Christ by the efforts of his people working unitedly, it follows that the only proper and right and safe place, and certainly the only strengthening place for every Christian convert is in the church. No halfway halting ground of desirable or durable character has been discovered, because it did not exist. The convert needs the church, and the church needs the convert that both may stand strong. If a converted soul feels that he has any claims on the Saviour, Christ, in just that proportion Christ's church has claims on such a soul. If a man belongs in spirit to the Lord's host and means to fight on the Lord's side, he will only endanger himself and confuse others by skirmishing independently in the citizen's clothes of worldliness. The only square and manly, as well as obedient thing to do is to put on the Christian uniform and armor and take place in the church ranks, if one really means to fight the good fight and keep the faith.

And why, in any possible ground of reason, stay outside? To love Christ truly is to do his will, not in this or that, but in all. The way of duty is too plain to be mistaken : Repent and be converted, believe and be baptised. Here are the three steps leading up to Christ's church and the entrance door of baptism. Why should any soul stand in the cold on the steps, exposed to the cutting blasts of worldliness, shivering midway between the gates of hell and heaven, when the door is open into the light and warmth, and sympathy, into the strength-giving atmosphere of the Christian's spiritual home—the church?

Duty urges from behind ; Christ invites from within. Do not linger in that worst of all places—the quagmire of a half-obedience. Get on the bed-rock of the church, the church of the living God, which is the pillar and foundation of the truth.

IN my citation of Wesleyan theological authorities prov-
ing that there is a special gift of faith which is not saving, I find that I have omitted some very weighty ones.
Matthew 17:20, he says, "This faith is usually called by
divines, the faith of miracles ;" and has been said to be a
supernatural persuasion given to a man, that God will effect
some supernatural work by him in that very moment. In
the present age, so far removed from those times when those
supernatural gifts were imparted, the subject is necessarily
obscure, and was, perhaps, left without farther explanation
because of the temporary duration of miraculous powers.
That a faith without charity might exist which should re-
move mountains, that is, effect things really impossible to
mere human power, and which, therefore, commanded an
adequate exertion of the Divine energy to produce the result, we learn from St. Paul who appears to have had this
text in his thoughts from his reference to removing mountains. But this faith, though it might not be saving to the
individual differed from saving faith only as it was directed
to a different object. Faith is saving when it is the trust of
a heart broken and contrite on account of sin, in the great
atonement, which is the only object of saving faith ; so the
faith by which miracles were wrought by the disciples of
Christ, was also trust or reliance, but its object was the
name or power of Christ, and this, undoubtedly, some persons appear to have possessed who had not the faith which
placed them in the state of salvation. It is thus that the

distinction may be clearly made between the faith which saves and the faith which wrought miracles." Tihs quota. tion confirms my distinction between the gift of faith and the grace of faith. Mr. Watson assumes that no man can prove, that the age of miracles is past.

Our next citation is from J. Benson's note on Matthew 17:20, "It is certain that the faith here spoken of may subsist without saving faith: Judas had it, and so had many, who thereby cast out devils, and yet will, at last, have their portion with them. It is only a supernatural persuasion given a man, that God will work by him in an extraordinary and supernatural way at that hour.''

"WE SHALL BE LIKE HIM."

E shall be like Him, oh, beautiful thought!
Well may our souls with rapture be wrought,
After the sorrows, the woe and the tears,
We shall be like Him when Jesus appears.

After the conflict in peace to sit down,
After the cross to be wreathed with the crown,
After the dust and the soil of the way,
With Him and like Him for ever to stay,

Never again shall the throbbing head ache,
Never again shall the beating heart break,
Never the task drop from wearying hands,
Nor the feet ever fail in the brightest of lands.

Never shall sin with the trail of its shame
Shadow love's sunlight, nor chill its clear flame ;
Saviour, oft grieved in the house of thy friends,
Ne'er will we wound thee when earth's frail life ends.

Death! 'tis thought does away with thy sting,
Makes us triumphant to meet thee and sing,
"Glory to God." When the Jordan is passed
We shall go home and be like him at last.

Master alas, thee we've often denied !
When the world scorned we have shrunk from thy side.
Yet, blessed Jesus, thou knowest thy love,
Pardon and help us with grace from above.

When thou appearest, oh, rapturest thought !
Well may our souls into rapture be wrought,
We shall be like thee when this life is o'er,
Wound thee, deny thee, offend thee no more.

3

THE BELOVED WIFE.

NLY let a woman be sure that she is precious to her husband—not useful, not valuable, not convenient, simply, but lovely and beloved; let her be the recipient of his polite and hearty attentions; let her feel that her care and love are noticed, appreciated and returned; let her opinion be asked, her approval sought, and her judgment respected in matters of which she is cognizant; in short, let her only be loved, honored, and cherished in fulfillment of the marriage vow, and she will be to her husband, and her children, and society, a well-spring of pleasure. She will bear pain, and toil, and anxiety; for her husband's love is to her as a tower and a fortress. Shielded and sheltered therein, adversity will have lost its sting. She may suffer, but sympathy may dull the edge of her sorrow. A house with love in it—and by love I mean love expressed in words, and looks and deeds, for I have not one spark of faith in the love that never crops out—is to a house without love as a person to a machine; the one life, the other mechanism.

The unloved woman may have bread just as light, a house just as tidy as the other, but the latter has a spring of beauty about her, a joyousness, an aggressive, and penetrating, and pervading brightness, to which the former is a stranger. The deep happiness in her heart shines out in her face. She is a ray of sunlight in the house. She gleams all over it. It is airy, and gay, and graceful and warm, and welcoming with her presence. She is full of devices and plots, and sweet surprises for her husband and family. She has

never done with the romance and poetry of life.   She is herself a lyric poem, setting herself to all pure and gracious
melodies.   Humble household ways and duties have for her
a golden significance.   The prize makes the calling higher,
and the end dignifies the means.   Her home is a paradise,
not sinless, not painless, but still a paradise; for "love is
heaven, and heaven is love."

CHRISTIAN WEAKNESSES.

————

THERE are many ways in which to determine the strength of Christian people. When we are brought in contact with the great works of charity and benevolence we say those people show their faith by their works. When we see an active, zealous, working congregation we are impressed with the thought that in union there is strength. We can estimate the comparative power of every congregation by the amount of work they do, and the spirit in which they do it.

We can in the same way, determine the weakness of Christian churches. There are visible evidences of weakness, and these show themselves in laziness and tardiness, and general indifference. It matters little or nothing what vital subject may claim the pastor's attention during the week when he is making preparation for the Sabbath services, when Sunday comes many can find an excuse to remain away. The pastor instead of preaching to a good congregation must be satisfied with what he has, and yet dare not in the least show a lack of earnestness in his preaching. He must be the same man as if every member of the church were present, and if he is not, soon some one will say he is losing his interest in his work. Here is manifested a Christian weakness. Here is shown how little sympathy the servant of the Lord has. Here is evinced a coldness and indifference which naturally weakens and enervates the minister. This Christian weakness of a lack of sympathy for the minister is not always intentional but thoughtlessness.

People little think of his heart-aches, but they expect him to think of theirs. They little appreciate his devotion to their cause, not that they doubt it, but are so because of a want of interest in his work. That is a weak Christian who lives without sympathy for his pastor. Again, another Christian weakness is that of shifting responsibility of work. All faithful Christians wish to see the work of the Lord prosper. But all are not faithful in this. While they wish to be in nominal relation with the church they want others to bear all responsibility of prosperity or failure. They shift every lack of interest on others, and ease themselves that those at the head of the church must bear the blame for this or that. This is childish in the extreme and shows a wrong spirit. This spirit predominates largely among Christian people, in which few are made responsible for everything. This might all be well enough if these shifters would then be satisfied with what is done. But let a little assessment be made for some purpose and how soon they arise to assert their authority. Let a little discipline be enforced by pastor and consistory and how ready they are to complain. They are unwilling to bear even part of the burden. Those Christians who shift responsibility should not be granted the right to vote in any of the ecclesiastical bodies until they possess charity enough to sympathize with others and grace enough to bear their part in Christian work. Another element of Christian weakness is laziness. This pervades the whole man and unfits him for any Christian work. He is satisfied if things are only half managed. He is contented with no preaching or poor preaching or anything that will not arouse him to activity. All he wants is to be let alone. He is a good *sleeper* for the church with one exception, instead of being under the floor to support it, he is on top to weigh it down. He is satisfied if there is no Sunday school, prayer-meeting, or anything else. It matters little to him whether the pastor has a congregation on Sabbath or not, and much less does he care whether the pastor is paid or not.   He sleeps just as soundly with five hundred dollars of a debt to the pastor, as if it were but a cent.   He is just as well satisfied if the pastor pays his own way to all ecclesiastical meetings as if it were paid by the church.   Sleeps just as well without paying a cent to missions as if he gave a hundred dollars.   Is just as well pleased to see strangers 'come to church and leave again without being noticed and invited back as if the contrary.   Would just as soon come in time to hear the benediction as the invocation.   He is just as happy if the church is locked up half the time as not, because it gives occasion to visit. These are some of the weaknesses of the Christian life. We would refer to more if space would permit.   May it suffice however to awaken some to duty.

THE ALARM CLOCK.

N alarm-clock not only tells the time of day, but it can also awaken people in the morning. Such a clock in my chamber set up every morning about five o'clock such a whizzing, and ringing that it waked me up. " What a nice way to be roused up !" some will say. Yes it is a very good way, *if I always get up when it wakes me.* " Why ? how strange !" you will say. Yet it is true ; my alarm does not wake me any longer, because I did not at once get out of bed on two or three mornings.

I have often thought that my alarm clock is very like one's conscience. Every person who knows God's will has such a clock in his own breast ; so that when he is going to do wrong, it gives an alarm, saying, " That is not right ; you must not do that ; God sees you."

But we must *hear* conscience when it speaks. If we stop when it says, "stop," if we do what it tells us to do, then we shall *always* hear it. But if we get into the habit of not doing what it tells us, after a while we shall not hear it at all : our conscience will become hardened, and we shall be ready to commit any sin, however great.

In the town in which I formally lived, there was a boy put into jail for breaking into a shop at night, and stealing money. This boy once went to a Sabbath school, and had as faithful a conscience, perhaps, as any boy who reads this page. But he commenced doing wrong in little things. His conscience used to say to him, " Robert, that is wrong ; you ought not to do that." But he did not obey the warning voice. He went on from bad to worse, until, as I said, he was sent to jail for stealing money.

Remember when your conscience tells you to do anything, *do it* ; and whenever it tells you to stop, *stop.*

SONG.

I Am a poor wayfaring stranger
  While journeying through this world of woe,
  But there's no sickness, toil nor danger
  In that bright world to which I go.
    I am going there to see my father;
      I am going there no more to roam;
    I am just a-going over Jordan;
      I am just a-going over home.

      I know dark clouds will gather o'er me,
        I know my way is dark and steep;
      But Canaan's field lies just before me,
        Where God's redeemed their vigils keep.
      I am going there to see my mother,
        She said she'd meet me when I come;
      I am just a-going over Jordan;
        I am just a-going over home.

      I feel my sins are all forgiven,
        My hopes are placed on things above;
      I am going away to yon bright Heaven,
        Where all is joy, and peace, and love.
      I am going there to see my class-mates,
        That's gone before me, one by one,
      I'm just a-going over Jordan,
        I'm just a-going over home.

I want to wear a crown of glory,
  In concert with that blood-washed band,
I want to sing salvation's stories,
  When I get home to that bright land;
I'm going there to meet my children,
  I know they're sitting near God's throne,
I'm just a-going over Jordan,
  I'm just a-going over home.

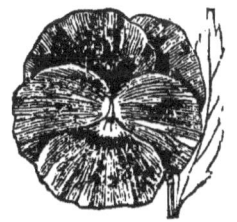

TRUE MANHOOD.

ORD Chesterfield once wrote: "A man who does not solidly establish, and really deserve a character for truth, probity, good manners, and good morals, at his first setting out in the world, may impose and shine like a meteor for a very short time, but will soon vanish and be extinguished with contempt."

How strikingly true! Nothing to-day is needed, we think, more than an exhibition on the part of people generally of those habits and traits of character which go to make up true manhood and womanhood. Not a few who are living in this age of the world are sadly lacking in these traits. They have, and exhibit, a part of those things which go largely toward constituting manhood and womanhood; but they seem to be deficient in many things.

What is true manhood? Perhaps we can give no better definition than that given by another concerning the true gentleman. He says: "The very term 'gentleman' has a flavor that indicates a fineness of nature as far removed from effeminacy on the one hand as from coarseness and brutality on the other. The ideal gentleman is a clean man, body and soul. He acts kindly out of the impulses of a kindly heart. He is brave because with a conscience void of offense, he has nothing to fear. He is never embarrassed, for he respects himself, and is profoundly conscious of right intentions. To preserve his self-respect, he keeps his honor unstained; and to retain the good opinion of others, he neglects no civility. He respects even the prejudices of honest men; opposes without bitterness, and yields without admitting defeat. He is never arrogant, and never weak. He bears himself with dignity, but never haughtily. Too wise to despise trifles, he is too noble to be mastered by them. To superiors he is respectful without servility; to equals courteous; to inferiors so kind that they forget their inferiority. He carries himself with grace in all places, is easy, but never familiar, genteel without affectation. His quick perceptions tell him what to do under all circumstances, and he approaches a king with as much grace as he would display in addressing a beggar. He unites gentleness of manner with firmness of mind; commands with mild authority, and asks favors with persistent grace and assurance. Always well informed and observant of events, but never pedantic, he wins his way to the head through the heart, by the shortest route, and keeps good opinions once won, because he deserves them."

This, it is true, is a somewhat long quotation; but it so well describes the traits and characteristics of what we term true manhood, that we could not forbear the temptation of copying it *in toto*.

True manhood always shows itself. It can not be hidden in those possessing it. Many to-day claim to be in the possession of true manhood who are really not. They have a few characteristics of manhood, perhaps, but unless they have them all, it is clearly seen that they can not justly make this claim. What are the traits or characteristics of true manhood? How shall we determine who have true manhood, and who have something else?

First, it seems to us that the person making a claim to true manhood will at all times and under all circumstances, *be a gentleman.*

By this we mean a good deal. He must be a gentleman in the highest and most exalted sense. He must not only *act* a gentleman, but must *be* one. "It may be a sham and pretense—hypocrisy expressing what is not felt—but it is a

good deal better to make it real, and then one is polite because impelled to be so by the warm, generous, kindly feelings that are within, and long to get out. Shams are dangerous things to deal with. It is easier to be a gentleman
or lady, than to appear to be one when you are not. The
best foundation for good manners is a real, loyal, gentle,
kindly, turthful character, and that is within the reach of
every boy and girl, rich or poor, handsome or plain, strong
or weak, trained or untrained." A true gentleman will
always be recognized by his manners, his politeness, and
his obliging habits. He will be known because he respects
the rights and feelings of others, and is always agreeable in
the society he enters. "Many a man owes his fortune or
his honors to his fine address. A man's success in life is
proportioned to the number of people to whom he is agreeable. He who has the most friends, and the fewest enemies is the strongest, and will rise the highest. A genial
manner disarms envy, and aid comes to its possessor from a
thousand unexpected sources. Unconsciously, and by the
force of habit, he has enlisted a host of sworn allies, who
help him fulfill his ambitions. Men seek those with whom
they can be at ease, and whose manners do not offend.
The young man who starts out in his career with pleasing
address is master of fortune without wealth or genius. He
is sought after and invited to enter in and possess. All
avenues to wealth and power are easily open to him, and
the prizes of his life are laid at his feet."

Thus is it seen how essential it is for one claiming true
manhood to be a gentleman.

Second. True manhood also implies that the person laying any claim thereto be in the possession of good *physical
strength.*

Too much stress can not be laid upon this part of our

theme. When the sacred writer wrote, "Show thyself a man," he meant a good deal. He did not, we think, confine himself to the thought alone that we should show ourselves men so far as morals and manners are concerned, but also in physicial strength. What the world needs to-day is men—men, not only possessing learning and experience, but also muscle and nerve. The day is not far distant when most men will have these great blessings in a very large degree. They will see ere long that they can not well succeed without them. They will see the necessity of having "*mens sana in corpore sano,*" — a sound mind in a sound body. Already, this subject is engaging the attention of our most successful educators and teachers. They begin to see the vast importance of educating the body in conjunction with the mind. The early Spartans (and in fact, almost all the ancients) saw the great necessity of giving their youth a good education in this respect.

The Spartans educated their young men in a stern and severe drill, commencing in infancy ; and, as a result, their bodies were made elastic, vigorous, and strong. Not long since, I heard a gentleman who was in poor health remark, that if he could only regain his health, and have the same strong body he had once, he would be willing to endure all the ills of life. Evidently, this gentleman knew the value of a good, strong body and constitution. He knew that so long as the body was weak and frail, the mind must to a great extent be impaired. "What single instance can do more to arrest the deterioration of our times, than connecting with our educational institutions some regular system of exercise ? The Gymnasia of Germany, within the last few years, have been doing a great work for that part of Europe ; and if, in the United States, in every school, from the primary to the college, and university, calisthenic and gymnastic exercises were made indispensable, and if in every city gymnasia should be established at the public expense, for clerks and others who lead an indoor life, what an improved aspect would the coming generation exhibit! The exercise of walking, riding on horseback, cricket, ten-pins, skating and boat rowing, are all of value." We are inclined to believe that in our haste and rush in the business of every day life, we too frequently forget that in order to have and retain true manhood, it is necessary, and very important for us to take a certain amount of exercise. How often does it prove to be a fact that all the real out door exercise a large number of us get is that we have in walking from the home to the place of business! Sometimes there are those who do not even get this exercise; for they ride to and from their homes. And yet, these self-same parties complain and grumble because they do not enjoy the health that others do who are good examples of true manhood.

Never need we expect to have sound, tenacious, and retentive minds, until we have as their abiding places good, strong, vigorous bodies. Then, and not until then, shall we be able to say we have true manhood.

Three. True manhood also implies that the person laying any claim thereto will be *a man of temperate habits*.

No one can have true manhood who is not temperate. If he is anything else but a man of temperate habits, he shows very clearly that his manhood is not sufficient to hold him within certain bounds. Oh, how many there are, who, if our conclusions are right and logical, are lacking in true manhood! Thousands there are in this country, and millions throughout the world, who are pursuing an intemperate course and showing to the world that they are sadly lacking in true manhood. When we read the statistics and see what a powerful sway intemperance has even in proud and fair America, with her intelligence and wealth, her prosperity and greatness, we are amazed and caused to tremble for the safety of a grand republic.   Think of the many hundreds of breweries in this country where a business is carried on which causes the destruction not only of all true manhood, but of the man himself!   How many homes are darkened and made sad thereby!   The evil resulting from intemperance is incalculable.

The story, the sad, sad story, can never be told this side of the grave.   God speed the day when such a great evil shall no longer curse our country and the world.   Then will this be a happy place.   Earth will be a paradise, and the name of God will be written upon all things; and both man and nature will unite their voices and praise him from whom all blessings flow.

Fourth.   But we must not fail to declare that true manhood also implies that a man laying any claim thereto must be a *christian*.

Although we make this the last qualification or characteristic, it is by no means the least.   A gentleman (adhering to the strict meaning of the word) is a christian; and a christian is a gentleman.   Until a man's heart has been changed, until he has had the blood of the Lord Jesus Christ applied to his soul, and felt that in very truth, "God is love," he still lacks some of the characteristics of a gentleman.   He still lacks that which gives to manhood its power.

A good description of a true gentleman is given by Saint Paul.   He seems to have believed a true gentleman must necessarily be a christian.   Says he : "Whatsoever things are true, whatsoever things are pure, whatsoever things are lovely, whatsoever things are of good report, if there be any virtue, and if there be any praise, think on these things."

Dr. Isaac Barlow, in one of his sermons, says: The true gentleman "should labor and study to be a leader unto virtue, and a notable promoter thereof ; directing and exciting men thereto by his exemplary conversation, encouraging them by his countenance and authority."

How true, the above! Well may we all covet such virtues. Having these with a few others, however, we may hope at no distant day to attain *true manhood*.

LITTLE PATTY.

CROSS little Patty sat under a tree,
As fretful as ever a child could be.
"Keep still!" to a singing bird, she said;
"You are out of tune and you hurt my head."

" Do stop ! " she cried, to a dancing brook,
A lamb and a pussy cat came to look

At cross little Patty beneath the tree,
As fretful as ever a child could be.

The Pussy cat wondered to see her pout,
And the frisky lambkin skipped about ;

But the brook tripped on over stones and moss,
And never found out that Patty was cross.

The bird in the tree-top sang away,
And these were the words she meant to say :

" You poor little girl, why can't you see
That there's nothing at all the matter with me ?

Mend your manners, my dearie, soon,
Or you'll find the whole world out of tune."

Somehow the wind in the leafly tree,
And the rippling water so wild and free,

The bird on the bough, and the snow-white lamb,
And the gentle pussy so mild and calm,

Made Patty ashamed of her naughty mood ;
She shook herself well, and said, "I'll be good."

And presto ! the Patty beneath the tree
Was just as sweet as a child could be.

4

THE JOY OF PERFECT LOVE.

WHEN love is the master-passion of the soul duty rises to delight—"we lose the duty in the joy." Duty is there, stern as ever. It must be. But when the heart is " dead to sin," and perfect love is enthroned, that which would otherwise be a burden or a task becomes a pleasure. The mother owes many a duty to the child of her bosom, and the little one by its very helplessness appeals for their performance. Yet the mother never hears the stern demand of duty. Her warm heart beats to the sweet melodies of a quenchless affection. She never thinks of duty while yet she is discharging it. And so with obedience to a heart that perfectly loves God. Nay, the Saviour has in infinite condescension used earthly rela tionships to teach and illustrate divine truths. And we find him calling the church his " bride." What does it mean? On his side it means that he "loved the Church, and gave himself for it;" that he loved human souls enough to die for each, a whole Christ for every sinner. But surely, on the brides part, it implies the perfect love that loves too much to serve from duty. Can it mean less? In every age and clime the bride and bridegroom have been the emblems of highest choice, deepest attachment, perfect love. And the moment that affection declines to mere duty the union is broken. It has given up its very life. The outward bond that still exists is but a name, a flower without scent, a cloud without rain, a well without water, a day without brightness.

If the church is the bride of Christ, perfect love should be her very life.

Yes, to perfect love obedience is joy. And it is a thousand-fold more exalted and Christ-like to have the whole stream of affection running toward God and obedience, than to have to fight an " enemy within," in order to be able to keep a clear conscience. Better to pray because I delight to, than because I must! And more beautiful to " work the works " which God has given me to fulfill, because the " love of Christ constraineth," than to have the task element as an unlovely feature in one's religious life, through not possessing perfect love.

WAITING.

I said, "When will the summer come?
"Mamma is it not late?"
She smiled, and answered, "By and by;
Be patient, child, and wait."

I asked papa if he would buy
    A new wax doll for me.
He pinched my cheek, and said, "Not now;
    Be patient, and I'll see."

"Nurse, tell me when my dear rose-bush
    A blossom red will bear."
O, by and by, my dear. Don't fret.
    Come, let me brush your hair."

When shall I grow so tall, papa,
    That I can reach your head?"
Quite soon enough, my little one;
    Wait patiently," he said.

"Dear me!" I thought; 'they all say wait.'
    I'll put my dolls away,
And go and sit upon the stairs
    As long as I can stay."

Now I have waited patiently
    For hours and hours and hours,
And yet the dear doll has not come,
    The Summer, nor the flowers.

I have not grown a single bit,
    And now I know it's late,
I'm going up to tell mamma
    It does no good to wait.

WORK.

" Six days shalt thou labor."

THE wickedness we are especially warned against committng on the Sabbath is work ; and according to the above command, the particular sin of secular days is idleness. Other commands to do or forbear certain acts are absolute and without reference to times or seasons ; we are not to suppose it is more unlawful to speak falsely or profanely, to take what is not our own, or to deprive another of life on the Sabbath than on any other day of the seven. Whatever is in itself right, is always right ; as, whatever is in itself wrong, is always wrong. " Virtue is its own reward." But work is not its own reward. We work, not for the sake of work, but for the sake of something else ; and we rest that we may be able to work again. Thus, neither work nor rest is in itself right or wrong ; only becomes so by God's special command, to labor on certain days and refrain from labor on certain other days.

The public conscience is often enough and with commendable zeal and emphasis addressed on the wickedness as well as impolicy of Sabbath labor. But is not the command to labor six days as imperative as that to abstain from work on the seventh ? If so, is there less sin in disobeying the former than the latter ? Is he who despises and refuses obedience to the law of labor less culpable than he who violates the law of rest ? Does not the positive command "six days *shalt* thou labor," as firmly and authoritatively set apart such portion of time to physical or intellectual exertion as the command to abstain from work on the seventh day makes the Sabbath sacred to rest? Yet the occasional transgression of the law against Sabbath labor is sure to be met with deserved reprehension, while the far more common sin of habitual idleness passes comparatively unrebuked.

But it is not only as a duty, as the fulfillment of an obligation, that the rightfulness of labor presents itself to our view; as a means of happiness, useful employment is of the first importance.   Industry is indispensable to the full enjoyment of life.   Willing industry rather, for, to work merely because necessity compels is slavish.   And yet we may well question whether they whose lot is hard, compulsory toil, enjoy less than those mis-called fortunate ones whose lives are a succession of idle, vacant hours.   Thousands whom pecuniary independence has deprived of all outward incentive to exertion and whose education has not taught them to find pleasure in useful occupation, become discontented, and unhappy ; and thinking the world would be better without than with them, wish themselves dead.   Give them something to do ; open to them a channel for their talent ; make them feel that their efforts are needed, that a career of usefulness is before them, and how pleasant life becomes ! how glad they are to live !

A SOURCE OF EVIL.

O one has studied either himself or his neighbor, or the Church, without having discovered that parsimony and spiritual progress are impossible in the same person. If a man have his heart set on money either to make it or save it, or both, he will inevitably dwarf in soul ; and if a church refuse to be liberal, and if it conduct all its business upon the plan of parsimony, it will dwindle and die. This is taught us by abundant observation and so plainly that it needs no argument.

We do not need to explain the reason of such a fact ; the fact itself is enough. If people will not profit by it, neither will they be profited by an exposition of law or a discussion of philosophy. Avarice and parsimony bring a blight to religion, and this being so, it is the duty and policy of Christians to avoid them. That they are not always avoided, and that they rule and control so many men in all their feelings and actions, is a sad illustration of the weakness of human nature, and of the power of a sinful propensity when it is not kept in check by grace and a healthy practice of piety.

There are many causes of trouble in churches, but more springing out of this awful love of money than any other. A man gives way to his selfishness and takes a stand on the side of illiberality. He gathers others about him and increases both the volume and force of his backward current. Sometime, before even he expects and almost before the others know, it has grown into an influence strong enough to disturb the peace of the people, and the progress of the work, and grace perishing out of the hearts of Christians, and Church work dying on their hands, they see the beau-tiful garden of the Lord turned into a desert and made the laughing stock of the scorners.   It is all the result of a pe-nurious spirit.   A proper regard for duty and for the inter-ests of the kingdom would have saved it all, and instead of the blight and desolation, there would have been cheerful prosperity and luxuriant fruitage.

WE MUST BE IN TIME.

BE on time for every call,
If you can be first of all;
  Be in time.
If your teachers only find
You are never once behind,
But are like the dial, true,
They will always trust in you;
  Be in time.

Never linger ere you start;
Set out with a willing heart;
  Be in time.
In the morning up and on,
First to work, and soonest done;
This is how the goal's attained,
This is how the prize is gained;
  Be in time.

Those who aim at something great
Never yet were found too late;
  Be in time.
Life with all is but a school;
We must work by plan and rule,
With some noble end in view,
Ever ready, earnest, true;
  Be in time.

Listen, then, to wisdom's call;
Knowledge now is free to all;
  Be in time.
Youth must daily toil and strive;
Treasure for the future hive,
For the work they have to do;
Keep this motto still in view;
  Be in time.

TWENTY YEARS OUT OF BONDAGE,

Or, the Intellectual March of an Emancipated People.

———

HE world moves, and the colored race of America is moving with it. We speak, of course, from an intellectual standpoint. No well informed man, who has watched the progress of the world for the past twenty years at least, will deny that he has been impressed with the fact that the colored race of this country has made rapid strides, intellectually, since freedom was proclaimed.

Twenty years ago, four millions of American slaves, unlettered and debased by centuries of oppression, were declared forever free. This done, the roar of battle ceased, the long night of darkness began to vanish, and once more the heart of a great nation beat freely as of yore. The crushing out of the rebellion, and the destruction of slavery, placed us, as a nation, upon the solid granite foundation of a pure Christian democracy, opening before us almost "dazzling vistas of honor, prosperity and greatness."

After passing through more than two and one-half centuries of oppression, such as that described above, the African race was allowed to go free. Our wrongs and privations had been many. Slavery had robbed us of much that is dear to any people. Without money, without education, with scarcely *anything*, save dear freedom itself, we were thrust upon the world to "sink or swim, live or die, survive or perish." What was to be our future we knew not. But, with strong, unflinching faith in the same God, who led Israel through the Red Sea, we went forward. Twenty years have elapsed since that memorable event, and what has been our history? How have we progressed? Have we proved to the world that we are men—that "we be brethren?" The united world answers, "Yes!" It is an encouraging fact, and one admitted by all who have watched our movements since the Emancipation Proclamation, that no people have made so great progress in so short a time. Sometime during the year 1871, the Governor of the State of Georgia, appointed a committee, consisting of ten persons, to be present at the examination of the Atlanta University. Said committee (most of whom were of the old slave-holding class) were in attendance when the examination came off. The examination lasted three days, and the following report was made by the committee appointed by the Governor: "At every step of the examination we were impressed with the fallacy of the popular idea (which is common with thousands of others,) a majority of the undersigned have heretofore entertained, that the members of the African race are not capable of a high grade of intelligent culture. The rigid tests to which the classes in algebra and geometry and in Latin and Greek were subjected, unequivocally demonstrated that under judicious training, and with persevering study, there are many members of the African race who can attain a high grade of intellectual culture. They prove that they can master intricate problems in mathematics, and fully comprehend the construction of different passages in the classics. Many of the pupils exhibited a degree of mental culture which, considering the length of time their minds have been in training, would do credit to the members of any race."

The avidity with which our race has sought knowledge during these years of freedom is remarkable, and it has been highly commended again and again. In so short a time one could hardly expect much from a people emerging from a bondage lasting two and one half centuries; but it is gratifying to the race, and astonishing to the world, to know that in the twenty years of our freedom we have produced Senators, statesmen, clergymen and doctors of eminence and renown. Furthermore, we have real estate owners, business men of keen insight; also editors and authors who are not only doing a lucrative business, but also giving instruction, as well as delight and pleasure, to thousands in the world.

Let us review the history of the race during the past twenty years, and show the moral, intellectual and spiritual progress made in that short period.

I. OUR MORAL PROGRESS.

It is indeed remarkable that a race of beings, debased, down-trodden, and abused for centuries, without refinement, without knowledge, should give so little trouble during these twenty years of freedom. When first set free, we made no attempts for having revenge upon our former task masters. We excited no insurrection, no mob, committed no murder; but at once sought honest labor, and endeavored to use the wages therefrom for the support and comfort of our broken families.

The colored race, since emancipation, has made a good record in morals. This is admitted on all sides.

A recent writer on the behavior of the colored people, since freedom was proclaimed, says: "They are of a peaceable, docile disposition, desiring to live in harmony with their neighbors." Mrs. McDougal, who is at present (1883) visiting the South, says of a colored school there, that "there must be great encouragement in teaching such earnest students. It is always pleasant to have good material to work on. Here also testimony is borne to the *good order, absence of turbulence,* and freedom from the scrapes into which white college boys are prone to fall, that has met me *in every colored school and college I have visited from the first.* Either they are kept too busy, or they have less original sin than young palefaces."

It is indeed a great wonder that a once enslaved people should behave themselves so well. Slavery, it is well known, is degrading to any people.

Yet statistics show that fewer crimes have been committed, and less trouble has been given by them, than by a proportionate number of free born men.

This may be owing to the fact that we are, as a race, "a quiet and inoffensive people." And yet, notwithstanding we have this reputation, the world has long since learned that while we are seldom if ever aggressive, we are, and should be, always defensive.

Is it not astonishing that, in the face of these facts, there should be so much objection to-day to allowing men of color to put up at hotels with other men, or to travel together upon public thoroughfares? Is it not strange that so much prejudice should exist toward a race of beings whom the world admits has acted so well morally during these few years of freedom? To day, however well bred or dressed a man of color may be, however little he may mingle with others of a lighter hue, there is no small amount of trouble gendered, and he is allowed no peace or comfort until he retreats to other quarters. Now, why is this? Is it because he has been a slave? he could not help that. Is it because he has a dark complexion? He could not dictate to his Creator as to what color he should have. Is it because he is not a gentlemen, and does not conduct himself in a gentlemanly way? This can not be the reason for such treatment to which he is subjected almost everywhere he goes; for facts go to show that during his freedom at least he has behaved himself in a most commendable and gentlemanly manner. On the public thoroughfare, at home, abroad—into whatever society the colored race has been cast, our behavior has not been that expected from a savage or enslaved people; but rather that of an obedient and law-abiding race in whom the traces of servitude could scarcely be seen.

II. OUR INTELLECTUAL PROGRESS.

That we have, as a race, made great intellectual progress in the last twenty years is manifest to all. No people ever perused the spelling book, and the reader with greater zeal; none ever seized the grand opportunity to learn with glader hearts. '' The desire to learn displayed by the negro,'' says a recent writer, "was perhaps the most surprising feature that grew out of his new condition. It quickly pervaded both sexes and all ages. Mother and child, romping youth and hoary age, attacked the alphabet and spelling book together, and kept up the assault with astonishing zeal. The number that has learned to read and write with tolerable facility is quite large; and there are few who do not make some pretentions to be classed therein." Rev. C. M. Southgate, of Massachusetts, says of the students being trained at the institutions in Atlanta, New Orleans, Charleston, and the other large Southern cities, that "the scholarship can be compared, without fear, with similar grades at the North. I never heard in our boasted common schools such recitations as I have heard from boys as black as the blackest. I know what Yale, and Harvard, and Dartmouth can show; but in Greek and Latin those colored students can rival their

excellence." Still another says: " They were turned loose
without a cent of their own or a letter of the alphabet.
That they have done well in acquiring property and knowledge under the circumstances, is the testimony of all who
know them."

But not only have we, through untiring zeal, acquired a
knowledge of the rudiments of education. We have more
of which we can boast. Many of the most responsible, as
well as the most lucrative stations in life are filled by colored
men — men, too, of no small reputation and service in our
country, and who "came up out of great tribulations."
There is Douglass, and Bruce, and Langston, and Elliott,
and Williams—men of almost universal reputation to-day.
Also others, whom we might mention, are making a grand
record for themselves, and their once oppressed race. And
what a noble army of young men and women of color is being trained in the schools and colleges that are scattered all
over the land ! In the year 1878, there were enrolled in the
public schools of the former slave States 675,150 colored
children. At the normal schools in the same year, there
was an attendance of 5,236; at institutions of secondary
education, 5,290; at colleges and universities, 1,620; at
schools of theology, 626; at law schools, 44; at medical
schools, 94. The deep interest, as well as the great faith,
benevolent people have in these schools and the pupils attending them, is shown by the following appropriations
made for their support. Maryland annually appropriates for
a colored normal school $2,000; Virginia for Hampton Insti-
tute, $10,000; Georgia, for the Atlanta University, $8,000;
Mississippi, for the higher education of our colored youth,
$10,000; Missouri gives $5,000; and the constitution of
Louisiana provides that there shall be for the same purpose
an annual expenditure of from $5,000 to $10,000. The

Religious Herald, of Richmond, Virginia, says that "in every State in the South the public school is open to the colored children just as to the white. Millions of dollars are raised annually by taxation for the support of schools for that portion of our population."

Now, these facts are encouraging to the race, and cause the members thereof to feel hopeful. Especially should this be so, when we remember that it is not many years ago since there was a great commotion in Boston itself over the fact that a colored child had been admitted into the public schools; and, also, that in the same old Puritan city the advocates of freedom were led through the streets with ropes around their necks. Thank God a grand revolution has taken place. Times have changed. The gate of knowledge has been opened, and all are permitted to enter.

Not only have our colored youth been enrolled as *pupils*, but they are *doing the work* assigned them, and doing it in a way that excites the wonder and admiration of their tutors.

Dr. W. F. Mallalieu says: "It must not be supposed that the young people in attendance upon these schools are dull and slow to learn. They average very well in all their studies, and will compare favorably with students of similar grades in Northern schools. The class in English Literature at Clark are at home in their examinations, and show the results of superior training, and superior ability. The class in Cicero at Clark can read Latin, and translate it with a fluency and accuracy really surprising. They catch the idiom, and the style and spirit of the orator, and show that they read in fullest sympathy with the orator. So other classes might be specified, and excellencies equally praiseworthy might be noted, but these will serve to indicate the possibilities which are within reach of these young men and

women who only a few years ago, were supposed by many
to have no capacity for knowledge, if indeed they belonged
to the human race. In a generation or two they will develope results which will more than justify the hopes of their
warmest friends, and amply repay all the toil and expense
that have been bestowed upon them."

It is indeed gratifying to know how deep an interest is
taken by the pupils in these schools in developing their
minds; also how much is being done to encourage them in
their pursuit for knowledge. What a grand work, for instance, is being done by the Freedman's Aid Society! In
the past fourteen years, 66,000 scholars were taught in the
schools of the society. Half a million are said to have been
taught by those who received instruction in these schools.
And, as a further illustration of what the society's work has
been, it may be said that it has aided in establishing and
supporting six charted collegiate institutions. Then, too,
consider the good work being done in this direction by the
American Baptist Home Mission Society. It has established twelve schools for the freedmen, and one for the In-
dians. These are supported wholly or principally by the
society. The total number of pupils attending these schools
to-day is 1,600. Of these, about 400 are preparing to preach
the gospel among the six millions of our race.

When these glorious truths are sounded in our ears, and
we remember the great disadvantages and barriers that lay
in our way, we can but thank God and take courage. Only
a few years ago, we were groaning under the "iron heel of
oppression," and considered fit for nothing but "hewers of
wood and drawers of water."

To-day we have among us doctors, clergymen, lawyers,
professors and editors—men of profound mental calibre,
whose influence for good reaches not alone the living, but

5

generations yet unborn. Not a few of our race have given to the world books, readable and instructive, in the past score of years, and they have received the highest commendation of the press. Then we have some eighty or ninety papers throughout the country, issued by colored men; and these are all ably conducted, and exerting a wholesome and widespread influence.

III. OUR SPIRITUAL PROGRESS.

By this I mean the advancement made by the church in numerical strength, intelligent ministers, and societies for the relief of the poor, and the promotion of the gospel. In this direction, also, we have made progress. Our religious privileges are greater, our houses of worship are more numerous, our church members are many, and many of our pulpits are filled with men of no ordinary intelligence.

To-day, there are in this country, 5,613 colored Baptist churches. Twenty years ago there were not half the number. To-day there are 3,257 ordained Baptist ministers. Twenty years ago there were not half the number.

In fourteen years the Freedman's Aid Society established in New Orleans alone 18 Methodist churches, and these churches now have 3,000 communicants. In the same length of time the same society established in the State of Louisiana, 114 churches, worth $230,323, and having 11,000 members. In Mississippi 300 churches were organized, and they have to-day a membership of 25,000. In Texas 208 churches are to be seen as the work of said Freedman's Aid Society, and the members are said to number 20,000.

Then there are hundreds of benevolent societies that give aid to the sick and poor. These also are exerting an indirect influence favorable to Christianity. Generally, the members of these societies are of that class who seek to do good among their race, and in order to understand the value of their service to the country at large, we have but to examine the reports of work accomplished in the last twenty years. In many of the churches, missionary societies have also been formed, and work has been done to send the gospel to the end of the earth. Sunday-schools meet once a week in their respective churches, and there they are intelligently taught the word of God ; and lectures, religious and otherwise, of a learned character, are given to the young and old alike, by some of our colored leaders who command an attentive hearing even among white audiences. What a change! How great a revolution in twenty short years!

In our churches we have, as spiritual guides, bishops and ministers of whom we need not be ashamed—men who have had the advantage of a superior education, and who are respected by all classes wherever they go. Sometimes we meet those who are surprised at the attainments of our leaders ; and they are led to ask the question propounded on one occasion concerning our Lord: "Whence hath this man this wisdom?" A case in point is that of Professor Ernest W. Clement, of Atlanta Seminary. He says: "Before I came here, I knew almost nothing of freedmen, except the dark side as pictured in Judge Tourgee's political novels. I knew very little of the capabilities of the colored race, and what I did know was not particularly complimentary. The day after I came here, I had an opportunity to attend a convention of colored churches. I must acknowledge that I was surprised, but none the less delighted, at what I saw there. I had never before been in a gathering of colored people, and their parliamentary precision, their orderly conduct, the intelligence and eloquence displayed in their speeches were to me remarkable."

It seems to be the belief of not a few men in the world, that the colored race is incapable of any great mental development. Nay, many appear to doubt that ''God hath made of one blood all the nations that dwell upon the face of the earth." But human nature is the same everywhere. Reports from all quarters of the globe, and from all ages of the world, make up a mass of concurrent testimony to verify the doctrine of a common, human brotherhood. Everywhere human nature presents but one organism. When Paul stood on the summit of the Areapagus, addressing the Athenians, he said God had made of one blood all nations of men. The brotherhood of man, and the oneness of human nature are clearly proved by the anatomical structure of man, by his pathological characteristics, by the duration of human life, and by the cardinal powers of the human mind.

Let once the deep sense of a common brotherhood be received; let it be illustrated in our lives, and society in almost no time will be completely revolutionized. There will immediately spring up among us a love and union that will prove as potent and lasting as truth itself. The injustice and wrong now and then experienced by the despised races will then be no longer feared. Animosity, prejudice, and hatred will soon give place to the wholesome influence of love, sympathy, and kindness.

Brethren, let us look to the loyal, liberty-loving people of this country for all that is justly due us. It is true, we have already much to be thankful for; but still we should not be satisfied until all our rights, full and free, are given, and we are looked upon as men and brethren.

We want, and ought to have, those God-given rights afforded citizens in general; we want, and ought to have, protection; we want, and ought to have, representation in national affairs; we want, and ought to have, whatever will tend most to advance our intellectual, financial, and moral worth.

These demands are right and proper inasmuch as we fought for our rights upon the fields of battle in the late war. Considering our numerical strength, and especially the time and labor expended, without any remuneration, in enriching yonder southern soil,—considering these things, we justly deserve a much larger representation in the affairs of this government. We have the men; and why not call them into office? It is customary for the nation to place those who were most serviceable and brave in the late rebellion into the highest positions of honor and trust, thus showing high appreciation of valuable service in the country's behalf. But how many men of color who were once brave and valient soldiers will be found in these positions?

A few directions as to our course in the future, and I have done.

First. *Let us be united among ourselves.*

"In union there is strength." Aesop, in his fables, tells of an old man who, many years ago, called around him his several sons. Having come unto him as bidden, the old man sent one of them out to procure a bundle of sticks. When he returned, the father requested his son to take the bundle, place it across his knee, and break it if he could. This proved to be too great a task for him, as well as for the remaining sons. Then the father endeavored to teach them that there was strength in union, but that divided they should fall.

So, brethren, will it be with us. Let us, therefore, see to it that we be united, that we stand together, shoulder to shoulder, in one solid phalanx. The age in which we live is one that calls for strong, stalwart men, especially among our own race. Now, "a single drop of water is a weak and powerless thing; but an infinite number of drops united by the force of attraction will form a stream, and many streams combined will form a river, till rivers pour their waters into the mighty oceans, whose proud waves, defying the power of man, none can stay but He who formed them. And thus forces, which, acting singly are utterly impotent, are, when acting in combination, resistless in their energies, mighty in power." So, too, is it with individuals and races. Acting singly and alone our power is little felt. But when once united, and we feel that one's cause is the other's cause, we then become one of the most invincible powers of the earth.

Second. *Let us continue our pursuit of knowledge.*

Knowledge is the great lever that elevates all nations that respect her. Knowledge is power. Where knowledge goes, civilization is bound to follow. As a race, we have made rapid strides during the past twenty years. This is the confession or acknowledgement of some of our most inveterate enemies. But let us not rest contented. Much ground yet remains to be trodden. Like Newton, we have been as children playing on the sea shore, and now and then finding a prettier shell than ordinary, while the great ocean of truth lies all undiscovered before us. What we want most as a race, is knowledge and wealth. Having these, we shall have all; for these two great earthly blessings, knowledge and wealth, will command respect from all.

Let, therefore, our preachers become more learned and eloquent; let our authors become more numerous and attractive; let our lawyers become more logical and persuasive at the bar—let the *whole race* diligently and earnestly pursue the path of knowledge, ever remembering that thus only will they become good, useful, intelligent citizens, and build themselves up to a higher state of civilization, culture and refinement.

CHRISTIAN UNION.

WHEN we examine the lively oracles of eternal truth we find that there was a unity and a happy unanimity in all the members of the primitive Christian church, that the whole company of believers were of one heart and of one soul, one in doctrine and opinion, being united in judgment and affection as one body animated by one soul, so that there were no controversies, jealousies, or divisions known among them. Their minds and thoughts were occupied about the doctrines of the gospel and the salvation of souls. They continued in the most harmonious manner to meet together in the courts of the Temple to worship God, and attended steadfastly to the instructions of the apostles, adhering to their doctrine in faith and love. Thus we see in them a lovely exhibition, and the effects of genuine Christianity. All professors of religion should carefully consider, and be disposed to copy, the example of these first fruits of the gospel—this specimen of the genuine nature and tendency of true Christianity; for unless their views, affections and conduct, in a good measure, correspond with it, they have good reason to question whether they are true believers, or are believers and members of Christ only in name. Every party, sect and denomination should study to copy the pattern here exhibited, and pray without ceasing for the pouring out of the Spirit to produce again such blessed effects among all the professors of religion, so that all may continue steadfast in the apostles' doctrine, and in fellowship one with another. If any professor of religion profess

that he walks in the light of the gospel as a partaker of
special grace, yet loveth not his brethren in Christ of every
name, it is evident that he is still in darkness, and a subject
of the Prince of Darkness, the author of all malice, envy,
murder and malignity.   Our Saviour's intercessory prayer
was that all true believers might be most intimately united
in judgment and affection, in doctrine, worship and love,
according to the mysterious union that existed between the
Father and himself.   As there should exist such a close
and intimate union among Christians of every name as
exists between God, the Father and the Son, not a unity
of essence and nature, but of will and affection, all Christians should have a unity of love, and of faith and
profession, a unity of practice and conversation.

In some respects this request is granted in behalf of all
true Christians in proportion to the degree of their illumi-
nation and sanctification.   But the more closely they are
united in judgment and affection, and the more entirely
they live in peace and harmony, professing the same doctrine and worshiping the same God as with one heart and
one mouth, this conduct affords the clearest evidence of
the divine original, and excellency of the gospel to the
convincing of the world around them.   For wicked men
are apt to say it will be soon enough for them to embrace
the gospel when its professors are agreed among themselves in what it consists.   Many professors are not aware
of the advantage which infidels and ungodly men have
made of the divisions and controversies among Christians
against the common interest of true religion.   But the
union which prevailed among Christians when the gospel
was first propagated, as springing from the communion of
the Holy Spirit the sanctifier, evidenced to the world the
divine origin of Christianity in a manner not much less

convincing than the miraculous powers of the same Spirit. All true Christians having a union and communion with the Father and the Son by the indwelling of the Holy Spirit should have a union of peace and harmony with one another, as this formed the substance of Christ's prayer to all his followers to the end of time. They can not see things exactly in the same light; thus a spirit of mutual candor, forbearance, and active self-denying kindness among all who love the Lord Jesus Christ, in sincerity, would convince the world that they are of one heart and soul, and are fellow soldiers in one army under the Captain of salvation, though not exactly marshalled and disciplined in the same manner, though they are all fighting not only against flesh and blood, but against powers, against the rulers of the darkness of this world, against spiritual wickedness in high places. All sects and parties should give up their party names and call themselves Christians, which name was given to the followers of Christ by a divine monition of the Spirit, according to the prophecy of Isaiah: "For the Lord God shall slay Israel and call his disciples by another name." Though the disciples had called each other brethren, believers and saints, which names were not sufficiently distinguishing, but the word of Christian donated their reliance on Christ, their anointed Prince and Saviour.

> Let party names no more
> The Christian world o'erspread;
> Let Christians of every name
> Be one in Christ, their head.
> Among the saints on earth
> Let mutual love abound—
> Heirs of the same inheritance
> With mutual blessing crowned.

Thus will the church below
Resemble that above,
Where streams of endless pleasure flow,
And every heart is love.

The whole Christian church, the body of Christ, the Christians of every name, sect and party, should awake, and with one heart and one soul go forth in one solid pha-lanx, unitedly proclaiming the gospel of the grace of God —the gospel of peace to the earth—and let all the petty disgraceful and ruinous disputes between the various denominations of professing Christians be forgotten, and put forth all their energies in one united force to the conversion of the world. Then the Spirit of God would be poured out upon the world from on high; judgment would dwell in the wilderness, and righteousness remain in the fruitful field; the work of righteousness would be peace, and the effect of righteousness, quietness and assurance forever. All God's people would dwell in peaceable habitations, in sure dwellings, and in quiet resting places; and the Lord would then comfort Zion and all her waste places, making her wilderness like Eden and her desert like the garden of the Lord. Joy and gladness would be found therein, thanksgiving and the voice of melody.

A PITHY SERMON TO YOUNG MEN.

YOU are the architects of your own fortunes. Rely upon your strength of body and soul. Take for your motto self-reliance, honesty and industry; for your star, faith, perseverance and pluck, and inscribe on your banner, "Be just and fear not." Don't take too much advice; keep at the helm and steer your own ship. Strike out. Think well of yourself. Fire above the mark you intend to hit. Assume your position. Don't practice excessive humility; you can't get above your level, as water don't run up hill—haul potatoes in a cart over a rough road and the small potatoes will go to the bottom. Energy, invincible determination, with a right motive, are the levers that rule the world. The great art of commanding is to take a fair share of the work. Civility costs nothing and buys everything. Don't drink; don't smoke; don't swear; don't steal; don't gamble; don't deceive; don't tattle. Be polite; be generous; be kind. Study hard; play hard. Be in earnest. Be self-reliant. Read good books. Love your fellow men as your God; love your country and obey the laws; love truth, love virtue. Always do what your conscience tells you to be a duty, and leave the rest with God.

THE CHILD'S ETIQUETTE.

THE following hints on Education, Etiquette and Morals, from the pen of George Francis Train, are worth noticing:

1. Always say Yes sir, No sir. Yes, papa. No, papa. Thank you. No, thank you. Good-night. Good morning. Never say How, or Which, for What. Use no slang terms. Remember good spelling, reading, writing and grammar are the base of all true education.

2. Clean faces, clean clothes, clean shoes, and clean finger nails indicate good breeding. Never leave your clothes about the room. Have a place for everything and everything in its place.

3. Rap before entering a room, and never leave it with your back to the company. Never enter a private room or public place with your cap on.

4. Always offer your set to a lady or old gentleman. Let your companions enter the carriage or room first.

5. At the table eat with your fork; sit up straight; never use your tooth pick (although Europeans do), and when leaving ask to be excused.

6. Never put your feet on cushions, chairs or table.

7. Never overlook any one when reading or writing, nor talk or read aloud while others are reading. When conversing listen attentively, and do not interrupt or reply until the other has finished.

8. Never talk or whisper aloud in a private room where any one is singing or playing the piano.

9. Loud coughing, hawking, yawning, sneezing and blowing are ill-mannered. In every case cover your mouth with your handkerchief (which never examine—nothing is more vulgar except spitting on the floor.)

10. Treat all with respect, especially the poor. Be careful to injure no one's feelings by unkind remarks. Never tell tales, make faces, call names, ridicule the lame, mimic the unfortunate, or be cruel to insects, birds or animals.

HOUSEKEEPING.

O NE of the best things about housekeeping is, that it requires the exercise of the highest faculties of the human mind; we see women every day who are statesmen in the management of affairs, calm, independent and self-possessed in emergencies. Some of the best traits of character are constantly cultivated.

If any class of women can be said to have virtues thrust upon them, it is the housekeepers of our day. If every woman would set it before her as an aim worthy of all that is strongest and best in her, to conduct a well-ordered home, a good deal of happiness and real beauty would be gained. How faces, once lovely, are transformed by the addition of those wicked little lines about the eyes and mouth which come from having fretted over necessary work—work, too, which, if properly engaged in, would not injure the doer.

There are times, probably, when the happiest wife and mother thinks with longing of Thoraeu's housekeeping at Walden Pond, and admires his resolution in throwing the fragments of limestone, with which he had ornamented his desk, out of the window when he found they must be dusted every day; but there is absolutely no use in fretting over petty annoyances, and since the danger of falling into the habit is great, every sensible woman will endeavor to look to the bright side of all her troubles.

Suppose the baked potatoes should be eaten the moment they are done, and an important member of the family, knowing the dinner hour, is late : don't worry over the matter ; every such little worry indulged in is like a chisel deepening the lines already formed by some real trouble. Everybody, it is to be feared, knows women who never seem really to rouse up to enjoy anything, unless it is a misfortune, and who remind their guests of the dinner Charles Lamb describes, where roast lady was served with every course.

SELF-INDULGENCE.

THERE are Christians, apparently sitting year after year in idleness, who profess willingness and anxiety to work if they could only find an opportunity for usefulness. Undoubtedly they are fastidious in their views as to the work they undertake, and mostly claim they lack the talent for any kind of work which does not approve itself to their tastes. The teaching of a class in the Sunday-school, the visitation of the poor, the making acquaintance with new comers to the church, the collection of subscriptions for missions or other agencies of benevolence, with other work which needs to be done, all present some feature which leads them to say: "I pray thee have me excused." The general disposition is for that which is easy and pleasant. But no Christian, giving the subject proper thought, can think such self-indulgence becoming. As Christ pleased not himself, the disciple ought not to withhold his service if the work which offers is not in all respects agreeable to his mind. If it is work for Christ, that should be enough to enlist his enthusiasm, and draw forth his best energies. Christian work is to be engaged in neither for pastime nor pleasure. It is worthy of self-denial, and oftentimes out of self-denial will come the grandest enjoyments.

BOYS OUT AFTER NIGHTFALL.

CHRISTIAN parents often make the mistake of thinking that their children are doing their whole duty when they are present at family worship, go to church pretty regularly, and attend Sabbath-school. With this they fold their arms, close their eyes, and settle back into the chair of security, and feel they can do no more for their spiritual welfare. This is, indeed, a sad mistake. Parents too often forget that a single word or act may change the whole course of human life, and fix the eternal destiny of the soul. The paths that lead from the home circle to the outer world should be constantly watched and well guarded. Those parents certainly do not exercise enough forethought and watchful care who permit their sons such indulgences as are certain to result in their demoralization, if not in total ruin.

Among the habits which I have observed as tending most surely to ruin, is that of wasting time in the streets after nightfall. I am a sympathizing lover of boys, and I like to see them cheerful and happy, and would not for the world say or do anything to cheat them out of their rightful heritage of youth, yet I watch with a jealous eye lest they form habits while very young which can only bring upon them disgrace and sorrow in after life. To permit children to be out after nightfall is to expose them to ruin. Under cover of night, mingling with evil associates, they soon learn to use bad, vulgar, immoral and profane language, indulge in obscene practices, and get ready to graduate in the school of vice as rowdyish, dissolute men.

6

Parents should have a rigid and inflexible rule never to allow their sons, under any circumstance, to go into the streets to meet other boys for social, out-of-door sports after nightfall ; but, instead, they should have pleasures around the family table in reading good books and papers, engaging in pleasant conversation and cheerful amusements. A rigid rule of this kind adhered to would soon deaden the desire for. such dangerous practices. But is this done ? Alas ! in very many instances it is not.

A walk through some of our villages and towns, late in the evening, or a visit to the stores and groceries reveals the sad and painful fact. There we find boys, from ten years old and upward, smoking cigars, engaging in idle conversation, jeering at passers-by, and what is still worse, they can be found too often at the saloons, drinking of the intoxicating cup. "What," methinks I hear some one ask, "not sons of Christian parents ?" Yes, I know whereof I speak. My own eyes and ears have seen and heard such things.

MISS PUSSY'S SICKNESS.

ISS PUSSY is ill ;
She lies very still
In her snug little bed,
With a pain in her head.

"O doctor !" cries she,
" Pray what can it be
That gives me such a pain
On the top of my brain."

Says old Doctor Grey,
Excuse me, I pray,
For seeming so rude,
But it is for your good.

"I really do think—"
(This he says with a wink)!
"You have eaten a slice
Too much of your mice !"

EAR GIRL:—How pleasant, how sweet is existence, this bright June morning, while every breeze
speaks hope, and the joyous song of birds seems
to tell of gladness in store for you; but does
there come no earnest thoughts of duty, no purpose
of faithful endeavor, and dreams of victory won through
patience? It is right that you should entertain bright,
glowing anticipations of the future, strewn with flowers
and golden with sunshine; but O, let the flowers be
kindly deeds and words of love, plants of your own
sowing; and remember that you have no time to lose.
As you sow so shall you reap, and though you will as long
as you live be still sowing, to reap for eternity, yet *now* is
especially your seed-time. Would that I could arouse you,
in some measure, to a sense of the solemn responsibility
resting upon you. Do not turn that pretty head away
with impatience, saying "My old friend has old ways and
old thoughts, and would spoil all my joy, by burdening
me with the thought of weighty responsibilities and solemn
duties. My work for the present, at least, is being
merry and happy, and just having the gayest time
imaginable. By and by it will be time enough to think of
serious things, and I intend to be good and wise some
day." Softly, my dear girl; the good Book says: "As
you sow so shall you reap." If by and by you would see
the desert rejoicing and blossoming as the rose, because
your feet have trodden there; if you shall have a right to
rejoice in time to come that "strength and honor are your
clothing," you should feel, even now, the stirring of high
resolve and lofty purpose. How do you prefer to be

regarded? As only a "fair defect of nature," or "the fairest of creation—last and best of all God's works," whose price is far above rubies? If the first, you have only to be a "girl of the period;" idle, vain, frivolous, and, in that by and by to which you are hastening, you will surely be that restless, most unhappy of all beings, a woman of the world. If you would one day be a "perfect woman, nobly planned," remember now, that it is only the fruit of your own hands that can be given you; your own works shall praise you in the gates, or be to you cause for shame and confusion of face.

I have heard of a young lady who is called "the merriest girl that's out," and spoken of by her young gentlemen acquaintances as "a perfect daisy—*so jolly*, you know." When she walks the street, she swings herself along, with an air of nonchalance which says, as plainly as words could, "You may speak to me if you like." She talks slang, and by conversing with her a half hour you may learn all the newest words and phrases in this department. If you see her at church (she goes sometimes, just for fun) your attention will probably be diverted from the solemn services of the hour, by her talking during the sermon; passing and receiving notes which she reads during prayers, and various other acts, which not only make her appear ridiculous to all sensible people, but which, considering time and place, are actually disgraceful. This young lady does not regard the wishes of her mother, and is almost daily guilty of false-hood and deception to evade the prohibitions of her fond and tender father. Ah! will not her sin find her out? Do you know her? Have you, my dear girl, begun to take up with any of her ways? Are you ever careless or disobedient to the admonitions of that loving father who would willingly lay down his life for your good?

TRUE WOMANHOOD.

A TRUE woman is one of earth's greatest and noblest blessings. Her price is far above rubies. Her presence in the world makes earth cheerful. Without her genial countenance, her kind and tender words of counsel, this world would be anything but a desirable place in which to dwell. Instead of the joy, peace, happiness, and prosperity now realized, there would be, without the presence of woman, sorrow, misery and woe. But observe, we say this only of the *true* woman. And here the question may be asked: "What is a true woman?" Well, about the best description of a true woman we ever saw, is the one given by the wise man in his Book of Proverbs. He says:

> "Who can find a virtuous woman?
> For her price is far above rubies.
> The heart of her husband doth safely trust in her,
> So that he shall have no heed of spoil.
> She will do him good and not evil,
> All the days of her life.
> She seeketh wool and flax,
> And worketh willingly with her hands.
> She is like the merchant's ship,
> She bringeth her food from afar.
> She riseth also while it is yet night,
> And giveth meat to her household
> And a portion to her maidens.
> She considereth a field and buyeth it;
> With the fruit of her hands she planteth a vineyard.
> She girdeth her loins with strength,
> And strengtheneth her arms.
> She trieth her merchandise that it is good;
> Her lamp goeth not out by night.
> She layeth her hands to the spindle,
> And her hands hold the distaff.

She stretcheth out her open hand to the poor ;
Yea, she reacheth forth her hands to the needy.
She feareth not the snow for her household ;
For all her household are doubly clothed.
She maketh for herself coverings of tapestry ;
Her clothing is silk and purple.
Her husband is known in the gates,
When he sitteth among the elders of the Lord.
She maketh fine linen and selleth it,
And delivereth girdles unto the merchant.
Strength and honor are her clothing,
And she will rejoice in the time to come.
She openeth her mouth with wisdom,
And in her tongue is the law of kindness.
She looketh well to the ways of her household ;
And eateth not the bread of idlenes.
Her children rise up and call her blessed ;
Her husband also, and he praiseth her.
Many daughters have done virtuously,
But thou excelleth them all.
Favor is deceitful, and beauty is vain,
But a woman that feareth the Lord, she shall be praised.
Give her of the fruit of her hands,
And let her own works praise her in the gates."

This is, indeed, the portraiture of true woman. She is described by Solomon most beautifully and minutely. She is a lady, and one that is not afraid of work. Yea, rather does she delight therein. "She worketh with her hands," is the language, giving us to understand that she engages in actual manual labor.

To-day, as perhaps never before, every lady is called upon to exhibit the traits of true womanhood. As man is called upon to show himself a man, so women is called upon to show herself a woman. The times demand this. Never has woman had a grander opportunity to make her influence felt in the world than now. And those who are not afraid nor ashamed to go forward, are being called to loudly by humanity at large. "In woman's nature lie the qualities which develop naturally into this saintliest ideal of womanhood, the ministrant of mercy to the miseries of man. Hers is the emotional, affectional hemisphere of humanity; and all her sensitiveness and susceptibility, her power of realizing by imagination the sufferings of others, her quick intuitive sympathy, her warm, overflowing dutifulness, her gentleness of touch and tenderness of tone, her graciousness of presence—are powers which fit her for this ministry of comfort."

There are many women who apparently do not understand as they should what is expected of a woman. They do not seem to know what power they have for influencing generations yet unborn. When we speak to-day of a lady, not a few women suppose that we mean a person of the fairer sex who is accustomed to dress well, and always appear well in society. They seem to picture in their mind's eye an individual who does scarcely any work, but who is expected to be found always dressed up, sitting at the piano, or riding out, seeing and being seen. But this alone is not the picture of the true lady. This is not the sort of lady that Solomon was so careful to describe nearly three thousand years ago. The lady that he speaks of—the true lady—"worketh willingly with her hands." She is not ashamed of work. "She maketh fine linen and selleth it, and delivereth girdles unto the merchant. Strength and honor are her clothing, and she will rejoice in the time to come."

What do you think the sweet word "wife" comes from? It is the great syllable in which the English and Latin language conquered the French and Greek. I hope the French may some day find an expression for the idea in lieu of that dreadful word *femme*. But what do you think it comes from? The great value of Saxon words is that they mean something. Wife means "weaver." You must

either be housewives or housemoths, remember that. In
a deeper sense, you must either weave men's fortunes and
embroider them, or feed upon and bring them to decay.
Wherever a true wife comes, home is always around her.
The stars may be over her head; the glow-worm in the
dewy grass may be the fire at her feet; but where she is
dwells the spirit of home; and for a noble woman it reaches
far around her; better than houses ceiled with cedar or
painted with vermilion, shedding a quiet light for those who
are houseless. This is a woman's truest place and highest
power.

What do we understand by "true womanhood." What
is that by which we may know a true woman, or, if you
please, a lady? In reply, we would say that a true woman
possesses several important graces, and we shall right here
mention a few, if not all of said graces:

A true and loyal woman is a lady in the truest and highest sense of the word. Wherever she goes, under whatever
circumstances she may be placed, her behavior is always
that of a true and refined lady. To all—the rich, the poor,
the low and mean—her conversation, her every action, show
that she is nothing less than a lady. Such a person is
loved of all. Her presence is light and sunshine in the
midst of any society. How great a boon, then is it to be a
lady.

*A true and loyal woman will delight to know how to do any
kind of honest work.*

Upon this subject we have already spoken at considerable length. But we must add a word more. There are not
a few young girls, occasionally met with, who say they do
not desire to know anything concerning household duties.
They seem to look upon this kind of work as degrading, and
not fit for their soft, delicate hands.

But we think they are greatly mistaken. They have a wrong idea of life. All work is honorable. And no young lady need be ashamed to go into the kitchen, roll up her sleeves, and there do the work that she may find to do. All young ladies, rich or poor, high or low, do well, we think, to imitate in this respect, the great and good Queen of England, or the true and loyal-hearted widow of ex-President Garfield. These women are not ashamed to perform any of the household duties. Moreover, they train their daughters to work, and urge upon the mothers of both continents the great importance of giving their daughters a similar training. Would there were more such women in the world as Mrs. Garfield and the Queen of England.

One thing that is becoming more and more manifest every day is the fact that most young men who marry in this age do not seek those for companions who have received no training in house-work, or who have looked upon all such work as mean and degrading; but in almost every case young men take unto themselves those who know how to perform the above mentioned duties, and who are not ashamed to let the world know it. Such ladies the world needs, and such ladies will ever be in demand. They are the ones who will prove themselves to be among the world's greatest benefactors.

What a responsible position do the mothers of this age hold. Upon them depends very largely the success in life of their daughters. They are the ones who should teach their children, especially their daughters how to perform any of the household duties. But we are sorry to say that not all mothers do this. Oftentimes they foolishly reason thus to their daughters. "You shall never do as I did; You shall lead a different life; you shall be spared all this." The parents of their daughters toiled and labored faithfully for all they have ; but, according to their reasoning, they desire their children to lead a free and easy life, and grow up entirely ignorant of any housework. How unwise! The day may come when those daughters will wish they knew these things. They may not have such a stream of luck, or marry such wealth as they perhaps think. We are in the world, but we know not how we are going to get out, or what we are coming to before the time for our departure arrives.

A true and loyal woman will make every endeavor at self-culture.

Not only will she strive to acquire a knowledge of household duties, but also to increase her stock of knowledge in general. She will give the greatest attention possible to the culture of her intellectual powers. A very able writer says, in answer to the question, what is self-culture? "To cultivate anything, be it a plant, an animal, a mind, is to make it grow. Growth, expansion, is the end. Nothing admits culture but that which has a principle of life, capable of being expanded. He, therefore, who does what he can to unfold all his powers and capacities, especially his nobler ones, so as to become a well-proportioned vigorous, excellent, happy being, practices self-culture."

Now self-culture, of course, has various branches. There may be self-culture in morals, in intellect, and in religion. Especially should every young lady cultivate these three branches. All are important, all should be cultivated. The time is coming, and in fact now is, when our young women will be required to fill positions of honor and trust such as they were not permitted to occupy only a few years ago. Young women to-day are attending our colleges and seminaries, and upon graduation they are frequently called upon to do service great and honorable for their fellows.

Let every young woman, therefore, feel it her duty to acquire a good education for self-culture.

Lastly, *a true and loyal woman will be unto the world a benefactress, a faithful mother and a Christian.*

She will be a benefactress. By this we mean she will be one who is ever willing to bestow a benefit, or favor upon her fellow beings. If she be a loyal woman she will delight and seek to assist all—especially the poor, the needy, and the distressed. She will aid them not only by her kind words of advice, not only by going among them and lending a helping hand in the hour of need; but she will give libererally of her means for the support and comfort of suffering humanity.

She will be a faithful mother. She will make it the aim of her life to raise her children properly. This she will do not out of selfish motives; not for the mere pleasure of seeing her chlidren grow up, marry well, and live in ease all the days of their earthly existence. No, this will not be the aim of the faithful mother. Her chief desire will be to do her utmost toward raising her offspring in such a manner as that they will be an honor not alone to themselves, but also to their country and their God. The true and loyal mother will exert all her powers toward training her children for a life of usefulness and profit. She will desire them to be a blessing not only to the living, but also to generations yet unborn.

She will be a Christian. If she is to serve the world in the manner we have just stated; if she is to exert a wholesome influence, not only upon her children, but also upon her future generations, it clearly follows that she must be a Christian : for none but a Christian can give the *best training* unto their children. Mark we say *the best* training. Others may give training, but all can not give the *best.*

Such is the portraiture of a true woman ; such the characteristics in part of what goes to make up *true womanhood.*

MOTHER'S GOOD-BYE.

IT down by the side of your mother, my boy,
　　You have only a moment, I know,
But you will stay till I give you my parting advice
　　'Tis all that I have to bestow.

You leave me to seek for employment my boy,
　　By the world you have yet to be tried ;
But in all the temptations and struggles you meet,
　　May your heart in your Saviour confide.

Hold fast to the right, hold fast to the right,
　　Wherever your footsteps may roam ;
Oh, forsake not the way of salvation, my boy,
　　That you learned from your mother at home.

You'll find in your satchel, a Bible, my boy,
　　'Tis the book of all others the best ;
It will teach you to live, it will help you to die,
　　And lead to the gates of the blest.

I gave you to God in your cradle, my boy,
　　I have taught you the best that I knew ;
And as long as His mercy permits me to live,
　　I shall never cease praying for you.

Your father is coming to bid you good-bye ;
　　Oh, how lonely and sad we shall be !
But when far from the scenes of your childhood and youth,
　　You'll think of your father and me.

I want you to feel every word I have said,
　　For it came from the depths of my love ;
And, my boy, if we never behold you on earth,
　　Will you promise to meet us above ?

MEN WANTED.

THE great want of this age is men who are honest to the bottom, sound from center to circnmference, true to the heart's core. Men that fear the Lord and hate covetousness. Men who will condemn wrong in a friend or foe, in themselves as well as in others. Men whose consciences are steady as the needle to the pole. Men who will stand for the right if the heavens totter and the earth reels. Men who can tell the truth and defy the world. Men who can look the devil right in the eye and tell him he lies. Men that neither brag nor run. Men that neither swagger nor flinch. Men who have courage without whistling for it, and joy without shouting to bring it. Men in whom the current of everlasting life runs still, and deep and strong. Men careful of God's honor, and careless of men's applause. Men too large for sectarian limits, and too strong for sectarian bands. Men who do not strive, nor cry, nor cause their voices to be heard in the streets ; but who will not fail, nor be discouraged, till judgment be set in the earth. Men who know their message and tell it. Men who know their duty and do it. Men who know their place and fill it. Men who know their own business. Men who are not too lazy too work, nor too proud to be poor. Men willing to eat what they have earned, and wear what they have paid for. Men who know in whom they have trusted. Men whose feet are on the everlasting rock. Men not ashamed of their hope. Men strong with divine strength, wise with heavenly wisdom, loving with the love of Christ. Men of God.

CHRISTIANITY THE LIGHT OF THE WORLD.

A SERMON.

BY REV. WILTON R. BOONE, OF SPRINGFIFLD, OHIO.

Text, John VIII, 12. *"I am the light of the World."*

NO man, who is at all conversant with history, will deny that Christianity has exerted a mighty influence toward causing the world to progress in morality, civilization, and knowledge. Whatever advancement the world has made in science, art, civilization, and morality is due chiefly and primarily to the wholesome influence of Christianity. Christianity has proved to be the great educator and civilizer of the world. Wherever Christianity has gone, there knowledge and civilization have gone too. These statements need no verification. We have but to read the history of those countries where Christianity has been received. The remarkable change there wrought is proof enough of the converting and renewing power of the Christian religion. It has been well said that "Christianity has wrought wonders in human society. It has elevated woman from her condition as a chattel and a drudge, and made her the companion of man ; it has removed the brutal sports which disgraced Rome in the very days of her glory ; and it has abolished serfdom and slavery from nearly all the civilized states of the world. It has profoundly quickened the spirit of humanity, checking the tyranny of princes, enlarging the privileges of the individual, mitigating the horrors of war, and founding everywhere the hospital and asylum for the more unfortunate of our race."

If one wishes to be more fully convinced of the prodigious influence Christianity has had favorable to humanity since its advent into the world, let him look at America, let him look at Europe and like countries where advancement has been made in science and the various branches of indus·try.   In what other but a Christian land will be found such high institutions of learning ?   Where else will literature and art be appreciated to such a great extent ?   What single country, without Christiany, can boast of her civilization, and especially of her literature, her agriculture, her manufactories, and her railroads ?   Not one.

I.   I propose to endeavor to show as far as possible that the present prosperous condition of the world is due largely, if not altogether, to Christianity as the light of the world.

When our Lord was here in the flesh, he declared *he was* the light of the world.   But just before his departure, he said, "*ye* (that is his church) are the light of the world." Perhaps this figure of speech was suggested to him by the natural sun that warms and illumines our earth.   Those who heard our Lord were informed by Christ that likewise he had come into this world as a great and shining light—the source of all spiritual light and knowledge.   Our Lord would have them know that he was the light and "sun of righteousness," the great central character of all history. Prophets, priests, and kings looked forward to that light ages before it appeared and shone so brilliantly.   They viewed it by faith far away in the dim distance.   To them, that light was everything.   Upon it rested all their hopes. They sang of it in their poems ; they regarded it as the greatest boon that could possibly come into the world.   And such, indeed, it really was ; for what, pray, would this world be to-day without Christianity? Had not Christ come as a light unto the nations of the earth, miserable would have been their estate. But God was mindful of our condition as sinners; and he sent the light in due time. To-day, the religion which Christ established is felt far and wide. Its healthy influence, moreover, continues to widen and expand, and nations that have made any considerable degree of prosperity in science, literature, art and commerce, are forced to admit that it is all owing to the renewing power of Christianity. It is recorded that a certain Prince was sent on an embassy to the court of the present, good Queen Victoria. The Prince soon noticed the prosperity with which England was favored, and he sought opportunity to ask the Queen to tell him the secret of England's greatness. Handing the Prince a beautifully bound Bible, she said: "This is the secret of England's greatness."

Now, it is characteristic of light to shine, "to beam with steady radiance," to penetrate its way into the dark places of the earth. Has not Christianity done this to a very great extent? Wherever it has been received, has it not proved a great and an inestimable blessing? Has it not been the means of the moral and religious elevation of thousands? Has not every nation adopting Christianity, found that their only hope as a people lay in its healthy and civilizing influence? Read history, especially that part referring to the state of the world just before the advent of our Lord. Hardly a darker and more oppressive age can be found. Wickedness and immorality were almost at their climax. The Messiah seems to have made his appearance at just the right time; for the people were almost ready to give up in despair under their grievous burdens. Daily, they were asking, "who will show us any good?" They had read and reread in the prophets that a Saviour or deliverer should

7

come ; and they realized that there was a time when he was much needed. The Messiah came. In the midst of this darkness and superstition, he suddenly made his appearance as the bright and shining light from heaven. The religion which he came to establish was received by some, and re-jected by others. Opposition arose to this new religion ap-parently with all its power. But Christianity was a match for it all. This new faith came from above. God was in it ; and in spite of every foe, the religion of the Lord Jesus lives to-day.

Now, it is remarkable how Christianity has triumphed during *these* nineteen centuries. Like a heroic general, destined to success, (whatever the opposition) it has marched on "conquering and to conquer."

In its infancy, Christianity had but few advocates. · But look to-day. Behold the contrast. What a marvellous change ! Wherever Christianity has made its way, *there* may be seen evidence of civilization and reform. Thou-sands, who once sat in darkness, are to-day working with Christian zeal and energy for the subjugation of sin in the world, and the spread of the gospel among all nations. Consider, for instance, what is being done by our Foreign and Home Missions for the conversion of the world. To-day there are in the Protesant world between thirty and forty chief societies, with numberless branches, who yearly expend not less than $8,000,000 on missions. The Board of Managers, connected with the American Bible Society, has lately given a report concerning the progress made in supplying the United States with the Scriptures for the fourth time. Reports from auxiliary societies show that, by their agents, 111,906 families have been visited ; 14,535 of these were without the Bible, and 8,104 were supplied, besides 6,944 destitute individuals. From the beginning of the fiscal year to January 31, the colporteurs have visited 288,718 families. Of these, 45,034 were found without a complete Bible in their homes, and 35,242 of them were supplied by sale or gift, beside 19,966 destitute individuals ; 25,810 copies of the Bible were sold, of the value of $46,521.79, and 37,336 donated of the value of $9,096.41 ; making a total of 163,149 copies, the value of the same being $55,618,17." Moreover, we are *credibly* informed that the Protestant Bible societies have distributed within the last fifty years, more than fifty millions of Bibles and New Testaments in almost 200 languages. What an immense distribution of the sacred Word of Truth ! And yet the demand is greater than the supply. This is indeed wonderful, especially when one remembers that two copies of the Bible are *published every minute*, night and day, the year round.

Think, too, of the growth of the churches of our Asiatic missions. In thirty years (from 1851 to 1881) the number of churches in the Asiatic missions increased from 81 to 550, and the members from 8,035 to 42,226. What was the increase in European missions ? The churches grew from 61 to 463, and the members from 3,241 to 47,046. What was the increase in all missions? The churches grew from 142 to 1,013, and the members from 11,276 to 89,272, an increase of nearly eight hundred per cent.

But this is not all that Christianity as the light of the world, has accomplished. Its mighty power is seen in a thousand other aspects. What, but Christianity originated so many institutions of benevolence and reform that are scattered to-day throughout the land ? What, but it, has influenced the world so largely, and caused it to advance so rapidly in the various branches of industry ? Why is it, if it be not on account of the wholesome influence of Christi·

anity, that the rulers of nearly every country receive it themselves and encourage it in their subjects? Why is it, if Christianity be not the light of the world, that in both Europe and America, the majority of presidents, and teachers in the universities are Christian men?

Surely, these things mnst be owing to the influence of Christianity. It can be attributed to nothing else; especially when it is remembered that no such advancement has been made in other countries where Christianity is not regarded.

Generally speaking, this is a Christian nation. By the people of this fair land, Sunday is respected as in no other country; also the annual fast and Thanksgiving days. And right here it will be seen that great respect is had for Christianity. While many, it is true, have not as yet embraced Christianity, the number is infinitely large of those who acknowledge its mighty influence for good.

Then again, it is significant to remember that our national congress, army, and navy are each provided with chaplains to lead in prayer, and administer spiritual food to those doing service for the nation. A like recognition of the healthy influence of Christianity is also seen in the various States of the Union — especially so in the Legislature, and in the schools and colleges.

Were we to go into details concerning the great influence Christianity has exerted in bringing the world to its present moral and intellectual state, we should have to show how Christianity has "elevated woman from her condition as a drudge; mitigated the horrors of war; checked the tyranny of princes; quickened the spirit of humanity," and abolished slavery—that barbarous traffic which, in this country alone, swayed her cruel scepter for two and one half centuries. All this, and much more, would have to engage our attention, were we to undertake to show *in toto* wherein Christianity has been, and is, the light of the world.

Were it possible for Christianity to be blotted out of the world, it would be seen in a short time how great a civilizer it is. This experiment, or rather, something similar was tried once by France. We are informed by a certain writer that "the French, after making the boldest experiment in profaneness ever made by a nation in casting off its God, and for a time seriously deliberating whether there should be any God at all; after madly stamping on the yoke of Christ, and attempting to establish order on the basis of a wild and profligate philosophy, were obliged at length to bid an orator tell the absurd multitude that under a philosophical religion, every social bond was broken in pieces, and that Christianity or something like it, must be re-established to preserve any degree of order or decency." And thus will it be with any nation or people that essays to abolish Christianity from the earth. " Blessed is the nation whose God is the Lord."

But there is another sense in which Christianity may be spoken of as the light of the world. We have been dwelling hitherto upon what may be termed the moral and intellectual influence of Christianity.

II. Notice now, briefly, its *Spiritual Influence.*

Christianity has a Spiritual influence upon the heart of man. As Christianity changes and lights up the outward world, so, too, does it change and light up the heart. It cleanses, it renovates, (or more properly God's Spirit does) and implants within the believer new desires for holiness and right action toward his Maker. Would you see the power of Christianity illustrated in a single life? Look at that poor, wretched drunkard. He has indulged in strong drink for, lo! these many days. Apparently, he has not a friend in the world ; but unfortunately, he has a large family who are dependent upon him for the common necessities of life.   Should you follow that man to his home you would see there a most affectionate, Christian wife whose prayers daily ascend to a throne of grace in his behalf. At length, after long and patient waiting, those prayers are answered.   The husband reforms, and is induced by his loving wife to become a Christian.   And now, what a change in that home where, but a short time ago, wretchedness and despair, poverty and want, were known !   The husband, wife and children now rejoice together as perhaps never before.   How many just such instances may be cited ! How many homes, once sad and poverty-stricken, now beam with radiant gladness !   How many hearts, once burdened with grief and pain, now leap for joy by reason of the relig-ion of Jesus Christ !

Christianity was designed to introduce into the world joy, peace, and happiness.   " Behold I bring you good tidings of great joy," said the angel to the shepherds.   Has not Christianity been a source of joy to the world ?   Has it not entered many dark places of the earth where sin and sorrow reigned with great power ?   Again and again it has proved to be the healing balm to many who were dependent and ready to die by their own hands.   Many have been encouraged to commence life anew by reason of the wholesome influence of Christianity.   Especially has the power of the religion of Christ been seen and felt by many upon coming down to the river of death.   To such who exercised faith in their Re-deemer, religion has been a source of inestimable joy in the hour of death.   They have been enabled to say with just as much boldness as did Paul, "O death, where is thy sting ? O grave, where is thy victory ? "   Ask those who are near-ing the river of death, if you would know the power of the

Christian religion over a redeemed soul. Question them as to its power to change 'the life and make it what God, in his wise providence, designed it should be—a life of peace and joy. To the oppressed and sorrowful ones of earth, Christianity is everything. As saith the poet,

> " It makes the wounded spirit whole,
>   And calms the troubled breast ;
> 'Tis manna to the hungry soul,
>   And to the weary rest."

In this nineteenth century the power and progress of Christianity are felt and seen more than in any period since the apostolic age.

"What imagination," as Dr. Haven says, "can forecast the conquests of the next fifty years ? The leaven is working in every land. The old empires of idolatry and superstition are effete and ready, to vanish, while new Christian empires are born almost in a day. Every new discovery in nature, or invention in art, helps to speed the gospel. Trade, commerce, revolution, exploration all prepare the way, and herald the approach of the heralds of the cross. This work of preparation has been long going on. Soon it will be complete, the initiatory steps will all have been taken ; then a universal Pentacostal season may be expected."

THOUGHT AND CHARACTER.

THAT which distinguishes man from the brute is his power to think, to reason from cause to effect, to investigate the laws of the material world, and to meditate on those great moral, and spiritual truths which are revealed in the word of God. We find some sagacious animals who can be taught to do acts very surprising and wonderful, but they can never be so educated as to perceive the relations of truth, either in science or morals. Whatever may be true in the modern theory of development, it is certain that animal instinct has neither advanced nor changed in all the historic ages. The horse and the ox of to-day are not wiser than their original progenitors that came to Adam to receive their names. The robin builds her nest in your yard-tree now, exactly like that which the first robin built in Eden six thousand years ago. The beaver builds his dam across our streams in the far West just as beaver dams were built across Pison, Havilla, and Gihon, those streams which watered paradise in the infancy of the world. Man is the only animal on earth who thinks consecutively, and proves by reasoning powers, and moral aspirations, that he is more than an animal, and destined to live beyond the grave.

It is an excepted truth in mental and moral philosophy, that men become like the objects of their thoughts and affections, that their intellectual and moral characters are formed by the things which most frequently occupy their minds. When a man engages with great earnestness and industry in any kind of secular business, excluding as much as possible all thoughts of everything else, he soon becomes known as a man of business mind. We hear of the scientific mind, the legal mind, the artistic mind, and other kinds of minds differentiated by objects of thought ; and not only is it true, that "as a man thinketh in his heart so is he," in real character, but his features are so molded by his thinking that adepts in the study of character can tell, with a considerable degree of certainty, the daily avocations of strangers by their appearance. Man sins and suffers, is degraded or exalted, becomes God-like, or devil-like, is blissful or miserable, through thought, and according to the nature of his thinking.

Because man becomes like the objects of his thoughts and affections we maintain that the Christian religion is indispensable to us if we would have the best intellectual cultivation, and God-like moral character. By nature we are sinners, and we can not be happy in our sins, as the whole history of mankind testifies. We must be elevated intellectually and morally to find the bliss for which our fallen nature is ever panting, and to fiulfill the hopes inspired by the God-given possibilities we feel within us ; and for the purpose of this elevation, where can we find a higher object of thought and affection than Jesus Christ? If it were possible to combine in one man all the merely human moralists of all the ages, he would not equal the "man of sorrows," he would not be worthy to stoop down and unloose the latchet of his shoes.

HOLD on to your tongue when you are just ready to take God's name in vain.

Hold on to your hand when it is about to place that to your lips which brings misery and death.

Hold on to your feet when they are about to take you into the place of sin.

Hold on to your heart when evil associates seek your company and invite you to join their revelry.

Hold on to your good name, for it is of more value than gold.

Hold on to the truth, for it will serve you well in time and eternity.

Hold on to virtue. It is above all price to you at all times and places.

Hold on to your good character, for it is and ever will be your best wealth.

WHAT CAN I DO TO SAVE OTHERS?

IN my judgement no converted man or woman should rest satisfied until this question is finally and prayerfully settled in one or two ways; either it is my duty to go to the heathen in person, or it is my duty to do the utmost to increase the number of those who do go and insure the success of their work. How many of those who are to-day hopefully saved, have ever asked themselves this solemn question—have ever considered whether God calls them to the foreign field or not? Who knows? Some of us may be to-day like Jonah, fleeing from the call of God, which says to us, "Go to Ninevah!" Were the obligations of the unsaved to the saved candidly considered by every newly converted man or woman, and were the matter weighed as one of individual concern, does God call me to teach this Gospel to the heathen, there would be ten to one for every home and foreign missionary. It is not necessary to go abroad in order even to evangelize the heathen, but it is necessary, if called to remain at home, to build up at home a missionary church. If I fold my arms and regard with indifference the condition of this vast bulk of the human race, or with practical heedlessness leave them to perish, I am perhaps myself yet unsaved. There is no piety in such a frame of mind and heart. At least one thousand million of souls under Papal, Pagan, and Mohammedan influence, demand immediate and earnest effort for their salvation. And inasmuch as a whole generation passes into the darkness of the grave every forty years, we have but little time to do all we are going to do, for a few years and we are dead, and they are dead also — both those who are saved, and those who are to be saved are marching silently, but surely to the tomb, and the awful unknown beyond! You who are to do must do quickly, or your opportunity to do is gone; and every day of delay removes souls, now living, beyond our reach. You must choose whether God calls you to personal dedication, or to the work of a missionary zeal and activity at home. You may choose if you choose candidly, but choose you must, or be a traitor to your trust.

You may, if God calls you to stay here, do just as much to promote the salvation of the world as though you went abroad, though not as directly. This last link in a chain is the one that is immediately attached to the staple, but every other link is equally necessary to the chain. If I am in my post of duty here, and am to my utmost praying, giving and working to fan a true spirit of missions, and save souls, I am contributing just as much to evangelize the world, as though I was the last link in the chain of agencies by which the Church is joined to the pagan people, and touched the very heathen by direct contact. The question is not, where am I working, but am I working, and in what spirit and faith? And since most of us are doubtless not called to take this place as the last link, let me practically urge each one to do his utmost to make the Church at home a thoroughly missionary church.

CAN YOU WAIT?

ONE important condition of success is waiting. There are processes in nature, in providence, in grace, which can not be hurried. There are things to be done which not only require labor and skill, but also time. No human power can dispense with this element. There are things which can only be done by those who wait. The whole history of God's dealings with man in the world illustrate this: "The husbandman waiteth for the precious fruit of the earth, and hath long patience for it, until he receive the early and later rain." There is no other way of obtaining it; he must wait.

The physician must wait; the disease must run its course; the wound must have time to heal; the fractured bone can not be made whole in a day. Time must assuage grief, and days and months must elapse ere the anguish of the broken heart is healed. So in the dispensations of God's providence, he who setteth up and casteth down, takes time to bring the beggar from the dunghill to the throne, and the monarch from the throne to the dunghill.

Under many circumstances of trial, the question is, can you wait? If you can wait, all things will come right; if you can not wait, all things will surely go wrong. Job must wait, while afflictions beset him, while friends accused him, while Satan assailed him; he must wait until God delivered him. David must wait while Shimei cursed, and while the zealous Abishai desired to go and bring the head of the "dead dog" who insulted the King; but David could wait, and did wait, until having gone forth in tears, he returned in grateful triumph.

In the grand unfoldings of divine providence we are constantly taught the lesson of waiting. Do we learn to wait, or are we constantly restive beneath the instruction? Can we wait amid wrong, until God the righter of wrongs, shall appear in our behalf? Can we wait until lying lips are put to silence, until falsehood has run its race? Can we wait while wrong-doers triumph, and iniquities prevail? Can we wait while we are misjudged, misrepresented. and misused? Can we wait while iniquity abounds, while craft and fraud walk triumphant, while friends forsake us, and while good men, deceived and misinformed, turn from us? Can we wait when friends become our accusers, and when enemies triumph over us? If we can wait with patience, we shall not wait in vain. He who has been the friend and trust of the helpless and troubled, remembers those who wait to know and do his will and he has a thousand ways of bringing judgment to light, and righting wrongs which his trusting children suffer. Wrong does go down, and those they have wronged go up ; lies perish and truth triumphs. The wheat and tares may grow side by side ; but the harvest is coming, and the angels are the reapers; and while the wheat goes to the garner, the tares shall perish in the flames.

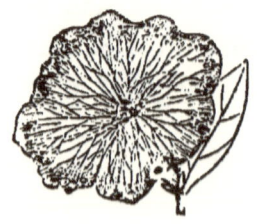

THE MISSIONARY SOCIETIES.

HE home and foreign missionary societies are the great evangelizing agency of our land and country. Religion is no greater system then man's duty to God. And when we look across the many broad mission fields of the different countries, we believe it will be gratifying to us as well as a duty that we owe to the grand mission cause in which every Christian should be engaged. For we are taught that Christ was a missionary, and if we are his disciples, we must be missionaries too. Christ showed his mission work when he came from bright glory, and suffered and died to save poor fallen men and women; that through his death and suffering, they might all have a right to the tree of everlasting life.

So it is the duty of every true Christian to work to save human souls, and also to save men, women, and children from the gulf of human depravity.

When we enter into the mission field of labor we are then in the Lord's vineyard, where there is plenty to do, the harvest is ripe, and the laborers are few. But we are calling for more laborers to come and help to aid the gospel of Christ, that his true word may be preached to every nation on the face of the globe. Let us work to Christianize and educate the people in the distant lands who are considered uncivilized; that such persons may be taught to serve the true and living God, in the place of worshiping idols made of wood, stone, copper, and brass, and here we give the

population of those different countries showing the numbers
that need the gospel of Christ.

POPULATION.

Africa, ...   200,000,000
India, ...   252,833,983
Asia, ...   50,000,000
Arabia, ...   12,000,000 to 15,000,000
China, ... 360,000,000 to 450,000,000
Japan, ...   34,338,514

The above names are only a part of the different nations,
who need the gospel of Christ and christian labor.   Ministers, teachers, churches and schools are all greatly needed
in those foreign countries; and in the different parts of
America with her 58,000,000, she needs christian labor.

MY OWN WAY.

NE day in London I wished to call on a friend residing in Guildford street. I did not know the way in
that forest of dwellings, but I took a map and saw
that from the Gower street station of the under-
ground railway it lay southward. I accordingly took my
seat in the train for Gower street, and quickiy arrived at the
station. In coming from the platform to the street, I had
lost my reckoning, for instead of turning south, I went
straight north. I felt, however, I was going south, and no
one could have convinced me that I was not. After going
a considerable distance, I thought I must now inquire about
the exact locality of the street I was in search of. I saw a
lamp lighter busily engaged at his work, running from lamp
to lamp, and I thought he would be very likely to know as
well as any one I could ask. So I said to him, " Could you
tell me the way to Guildford street ? "

"You are a good way from it. Go right back this street,
go past the Gower street station, keep straight on, and then
inquire."

"That's odd," said I, "is not this the way ? " still feeling
I was quite right, and the lamplighter was wrong ; but he
very patiently tried to convince me, and said :

"If you go on this way, you get away into Camden Town,
quite the opposite direction you wish ; but go straight back,
and you'll find your place."

But, as the popular phrase is, "my head was turned," and
nothing would convince me that my feelings were wrong.

8

and the lamplighter right. I was quite sure I was going south."

"Well," I said, "I can't understand it; the way you point seems to me to be going away from the direction I wish to go, and this way I'm going seems to be right."

The patient lamplighter had to be at his work, and had no time to stop and argue with one who seemed so hard to be convinced, so he said:

"Well, sir, of course, if you know better than I do, then it's all right. Just go on and take your own road."

He went away I have no doubt highly amused at my dilemma, and I stood reasoning on what the lamplighter had *said*, and what I *felt*. "I wonder if he is correct? Does he not mean to deceive me? I feel he is wrong." And my feeling's prevailed over the lamplighter's arguments. I went on, therefore, in my own way for a considerable distance, till I saw a policeman. "Now," I thought, "I'll ask again." But I unconsciously put my question to him, letting him see in what direction I wished the sought-for street to be.

"Isn't this straight for Guildford street?"

"Yes, just straight on, more than half a mile," said the policeman, who, I believe knew nothing about where it was, but not wishing to show his ignorance, and taking his cue from my question, gave me the wrong directions, and strengthened me in my conviction that I was going right.

I therefore kept on my way, turning over in my mind the testimony of the lamplighter, and my own feeling, backed by the testimony of the policeman, until I got confused, and did not know which to believe. If I am wrong, I thought, every step I am taking is leading me farther and farther from the place, and time is precious. If I am right, it would do no harm to ask again. I remembered that the British Museum was in the vicinity of Guildford street, and would be better known, so I asked a respectable looking young man, whom I met, "Which is the way to the British Museum ? "

"Straight back the way you have come, till you reach Gower street, cross the Euston road, and onward, and then inquire."

His answer was so straight, and his way of putting it so positive, and coinciding as it did in every point with the lamplighter's testimony, that without a moment's hesitation, I threw overboard the policeman's doubtful witness and my own feeling, and began, in no enviable frame of mind, to retrace my wearied steps, and in due time I found my destination, and thus proved the truth of the two true witnesses, the lamplighter and the young man, and got a good lesson that truthful testimony is a much safer guide than doubtful feelings.

By nature, every man is going in the wrong way, for "we have turned every one to his own way." Many think, that though not quite safe, still they are in the right way, and only need a little help to speed them on. A little religion, a little prayer, a little self sacrifice, a little reformation, and they feel quite comfortable—they feel they are, at least, attempting to do their duty, and if they fail it will be very singular. They educate themselves into this thought, until it becomes part of their being, and no testimony is heard but that which confirms their preconceived idea. A faithful witness who tells the downright, honest, unvarnished truth, that the only way is ' to the right about," is disbelieved and unheeded.

If there has not been a time in your history, where you have come to a stand still, to a dead halt, and throwing overboard your own feelings, your own preconceived notions, and the testimony of the majority of people around you,

you have started simply and entirely upon the testimony of God—his testimony concerning Christ as "the way "—his testimony concerning a finished work—his testimony concerning your perfect acceptance in Christ—there is grave reason for fearing that every step you are taking is away from God. You may not know the minute, the hour, day, or month, but do know the *fact?* Can you say, "Whereas I was blind, now I see?"

The world, the devil and the flesh will all cheat you and mislead you. You have no friend but God. But he is your friend, a real friend of sinners, and you are one, whether you feel it or not. You can not trust yourself. You can not trust your own feelings. God can not trust you, and he does not now intend, but he says, "Will you trust me?" He has done everything to secure your confidence. He so loved you that he gave you Christ, who came and put away sin, and so made a righteous channel through which his love might flow. He hath sent down the Holy Ghost to tell you of the finished and accepted work—that "all things are now ready," that the door is open, the feast spread, and you are heartily welcome. Merely appropriate all. Do not *try* to believe, nor to *feel* something, but simply stand still, take God at his word, against every other testimony, trust Christ as yours, and then begin your heavenward course as a child of God.

Luther, I think, used to say that Satan sometimes tempted him, and said, " Do you feel, Martin Luther, that you are saved ? "

" No," said Luther, "but I am sure of it."

Why? Because he believed God's testimony, and not his own changing feeling.

If you stand and look toward the sun, moon or stars, you do not feel that the earth moves ; you are rather inclined to believe that the heavens go round the earth ; and so the ancients believed, but it is a mistake. We believe what we do not feel—the earth goes round the sun.

"If we receive the witness of men, the witness of God is greater." And his witness is all about his Son.

If you persist in keeping your own way, instead of accepting God's Christ and his salvation, God must say, after you reject light, Take your own way, see where it will end. Prov. i, 31. What an end! Away from God forever !—the wrath of God weighing you down forever !—the flames of hell torturing soul and body forever !—but we beseech you now, on the spot, before you lay down this paper, stand and tell God that you are wrong ; tell him you have not been converted ; tell him you need his salvation, you need his Christ ; thank him for his Christ ; tell him you believe what he says, and this is what he says, that he "hath given to us eternal life, and this life is in his Son." John v. 11.

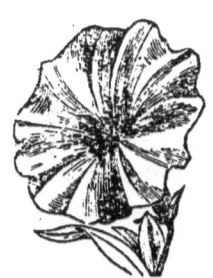

THE CHURCH AND THE WORD.

HE Church and the Bible are the centers or sources of the two greatest manifest moral forces in the world. They supplement each other. Neither could do without the other. It would be impossible for the Church to subsist in its present form, and do the work which is committed to it, were it deprived of the Bible. On the other hand, the Bible would be without influence or power to control human thought, if it were not brought to the homes and hearts of men by the agency of ·the Church.

The Bible is a book containing the revealed will of God, given by the inspiration of the Holy Spirit, continued through many generations, and by the ministry of many different men. The Church is an illustration of the spirit and principles of the book. The Bible is the repository of Divine truth; the Church is the manifestation of the power of Divine truth to bless and save all who really receive it. Both the Bible and the Church are witnesses for God, in the midst of a benighted, sinful, rebellious world.

The Bible as the repository of Divine truth, has held, all through the generations, the only written communication which has ever emanated from the court of Heaven to the dwellers upon this earth. Long before- the advent of Christ, this wonderful Book was commenced, and God made known His will to men, and caused it to be recorded in a permanent form. And since the second canon was closed, and the Bible has been in the hands of men as a complete book, it has been true to its mission. All through the dark ages, when worldiness and corruption had well nigh destroyed the spiritual life and power of Christianity, the Bible still held the unadulterated truth of God. More than this, it may be said that the Bible was the means of awakening a backslidden Church.

It was the Bible so read by Wickliffe, and Huss, and Jerome, and Martin Luther, that more than anything else, and more than all things else, moved these men so mightily, and sent them forth to battle with sin and superstition. Had it not been for the Bible, their hearts would never have been stirred to the proclamation of the truth; the Church would never have been aroused; sin would never have been rebuked; the chains of superstition would never have been broken ; and the world never would have felt the magnificent up-lift towards God and Heaven. And just so surely as the awakening of the past has shown the result of the influence of the Bible, so surely is the real progress of the future dependent upon the same source of spiritual power. There may be convulsions and revolutions and destructions without end, but there will never be a healthy, world-wide progress, except as the principles of the Bible shall prevail. All reforms and reformers who ignore the Bible will eventually prove to be utter and ignominious failures. The Bible, among all the books, is humanity's only hope.

Besides, we must remember that the Bible alone, of all the books that have ever been written, answers all questions of the soul. It is affirming much, but none too much, when it is said that this Bible answers every problem connected with man's relations to time and eternity, in so far as is necessary for his highest well-being and happiness. Here we find the true significance of life, here the veil is lifted from the future, here life and immortality are brought to light. The most terrible mystery of the universe, sin, is met with provisions for its perfect cure, while the grave and death are made radiant with the light of a most glorious hope. No philosophies of men have ever so appealed to all that is grandest and best in human nature, as this Book, and no other so completely satisfies the aspirations and questionings of our souls.

It only needs that the Church should more and more conform itself to the teachings of the Bible in order to realize the sublimest moral victories that have entered the mind of man to imagine. The Church must have the purity which the Bible teaches; it must take hold of all genuine reforms, and push them forward; it must have more practical righteousness, integrity, honor, honesty; it must have a more intense sympathy with Christ for the conversion of the world; it must never forget that it is militant, and not triumphant, that it must be more aggressive in its work of spreading the truth, and more aggressive in its conflict with the sin-force of this present age; and above all, it must have the baptism of fire and the Holy Ghost. Then, with the Bible as its standard of faith and morals, it may go forth to the conquest of this world. Oh that God would help the Church to come up to the Bible ideal, and so hasten the final advent of the Lord Jesus Christ!

SCRIPTURE LESSONS.

To preach a gospel sermon. Preaching means—To discourse publicly on religious subjects.

The word gospel means—Glad tidings concerning Christ, and salvation through him, any system of religious truth or doctrine, which is warning against every rising evil of the land — for the sake of Christ our Lord.

A sermon means a discourse or a text on scripture, explaining the declaration of Christ which pertains to general good over all evil.

By reading the Bible, we find the duty of man and woman through life under two heads. Under one is what we should not do, and the other one is what we must do, —which refers more especially to professed Christians. There is a certain amount of work assured to the hand of every professed Christian to do, something to help save the souls, lives and characters of other persons as well as to work, to sustain their own souls and bodies. We must remember that religion consists of not only faith alone, but faith and works, which do constitute the religion.

The duty of every christian is to work to keep peace and union among themselves, in order that they may set that peaceful example, that the world may follow.

WE TAKE THE BIBLE FOR OUR GUIDE.

Moreover if thy brother shall trespass against thee, go and tell him his faults between thee and him alone; if he shall hear thee, thou hast gained thy brother.

But if he will not hear thee, then take with thee one or two more, that in the mouth of two or three witnesses every word may be established.

And if he shall neglect to hear them, tell it unto the church ; but if he neglect to hear the church, let him be unto thee as an heathen man and a publican. Matthew, 18th chapter, 15th, 16th, and 17th verses.

Every person is in this world for an express purpose. God has given to every human a talent with human knowledge to improve that talent. And men and women who have improved their talent and intellect, combined with their education, are duty bound to use their education in every direction, which may be for the elevation and general good of their fellow man, and also to help the advancement of this world that it may be made better. All educators among men and women, should set the example in using their talent in trying to make good, grand, and beautiful the world's many wonders, so that heaven may be its ending.

We are taught by the scriptures that one christian can chase a thousand sinners, and two can put ten thousand to flight. While this is true we can see what great power there is in Christianity.

THE DUTY OF THE HUSBAND TO THE WIFE.

FIRST, the husband should love his wife and obey her, just so far as she has power as a wife, especially over her household affairs, and never neglect the society of the wife, and should not fail to regard her as his equal. Let the husband esteem and adore his wife above all other living women, and treat her with the greatest of kindness; have but very little to do with her household affairs, unless you are trying to advise her for the better; and, as husband, always talk and act so as to make the wife feel that you are her nearest friend; and forbid her working out from home at daily labor, unless she is compelled; and as a protecting husband he will give his wife to understand that he stands head, and he will do the supporting, while she must stay at home and keep house, and work to save what he makes, and do her part of the work at home; and he, as a good man, will keep her supplied with some little money, change, for the purpose of getting little notions and other small articles, that ladies like to purchase at times. And the husband must remember, too, that he can not consult a counsellor more deeply interested in his welfare than his true, devoted wife. And he should never fail to adhere to her good advice when he knows her to be in the right. For it's a well known fact that the advice of good women have saved thousands of men from destruction, one way or the other. And the good husband should, at all times, be ready to admonish and speak to his wife kind and consoling words. And if the husband happens to be a wicked, swearing man, he should be very careful to never swear or make use of any improper language in the presence of his wife or children. The kind husband will try to avoid quarrels and disputes, and, if necessary, he will try to reason with the wife, and if he happens to get a little angry at times he must hold his temper from her, for the sake of peace in the family, and will do all in his power for the happiness of the wife.

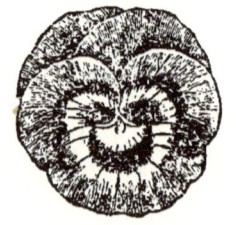

DUTY OF THE WIFE TO THE HUSBAND.

HE duty of the wife to the husband is, to first honor and obey him in all things which she knows to be just and right; which she thinks will be pleasing to him. And when she finds her husband in the wrong she should admonish him, and give her good advice to him for the better. And the good wife should be watchful that nothing in her conduct or conversation detracts from the happiness of sweet home. She must greatfully reciprocate the kindness and the attention of her husband, and sympathize with him in all that may be pertaining to the happiness of man and wife. And the woman will be a help-mate to her husband, according to the will of God, and she must be a partner of his joys and sorrow. Let his joy be her joy, and when he sorrows she must sorrow, and never fail to be his comforter in affliction, and the chief delight of his prosperity. The good wife knows it to be the business of every lawful married woman to strive to make their homes happy, and the wife shall be careful to treat her husband with all kindness, and it matters not how angry she may get, at times, she should never lose her temper, for fear she might speak words that would cause trouble in the family, while at the same time there can be peace and good will; of course, when she, as a wife, knows that her husband is laboring each day for the support of her and her children; and, as a wife, she should be very careful that she entertains with kindness and courtesy her husband's friends, and if she should see that his friends are dear to him, they should be dear to her; and her good sense will always prevent her from trying to rule her husband, for she knows that such conduct would be somewhat degrading to both parties; and if the husband should object to his wife being away from home at times, and attending too often these different entertainments, she should quickly obey him and be contented to stay at home, in case that he may know better what is best for her, and that her husband may be pleased. The good wife should never say to her husband that she will go when she pleases, and where she pleases, and stay as long as she pleases.   But still we are glad to know that every sensible and lawful married lady knows that such conduct, for a wife, is so unpleasant that it creates strife in the family, which may quickly throw back the large folding doors for a sad separation between the parties.   The intelligent and industrious ladies will never seek to marry a man for his pretty face—for beauty itself will be no comfort to the suffering wife in time of need; and every lady and gentleman knows that beauty resembles the bright blooming sunflower.   But very soon it fades and is cut down, to go like the withered grass.   And if the wife meddles with her husband's affairs, let the same be in the way of good advice.

THE PASSION OF LOVE.

WE notice that there are two kinds of love, one is spiritual, and the other temporal. Spiritual love was revealed to man's heart through the shed blood of Christ our Lord, which compels both men and women to strive to live in accordance with the will of God. Charity for all and malace toward none. You will love your neighbor as yourself. Temporal love is created by human nature. Persons will love their husbands and wives, fathers, mothers, and children, while there are other persons without love for husband and wife, and other relation, but neither have more affection for outside friends, and great love for strangers on the first sight.

But we find that love in the more common acceptation of the term is a bond of attachment between individuals of the different sexes, and is the emotion that is raised by qualities in the object which excites the highest pleasurable sensation; it is the ardent affection of man for woman — the affection of woman for man. Love is the soul of virtue; the divinity that stirs within man; the passions and the affections of the human minds, were all designed for good. But I believe that love passions are little bad for some people, when one person has to wag the whole burden for both parties, and at the same time we must remember that love has a language of its own, and will thank no book of etiquette for a lesson, or any outside person for advice. If the lady will be particularly modest in all her ways, and the gentleman will only be manly and sincere in all his word and conversations to her, they will appreciate and understand each other, without danger of making any mistakes on the part of their love. So I am forced to believe that a woman makes a mistake, and a large one too, when she depends upon the love she has for the man to carry her through life, because the gentleman whom she might choose to be her wedded husband, by the way of love, the same man might prove himself as nothing but a drunkard with a demoralized character, and subject to all bad habits ; or he might prove to be a gentleman of integrity and sobriety, and worthy of a good, honest wife. From the above facts, we go on to show that love is only of itself, especially on the part of the woman ; for she can love the man all she wants to, and as hard as she pleases. But just her love for him alone, will never furnish her a house for shelter, and provide for her food and raiment. Let the unmarried woman be careful to first seek the love of an honest, sober, intelligent, industrious and peaceable gentlemen to be her wedded husband for life, and if successful, there the lady shall center her affection.

And the gentleman on the other hand should first seek and find the lady to be honest hearted, virtuous, intelligent, and an industrious christian lady, before he should be too hasty about centering his affection upon her as his companion for life. And let us remember too that true love is one of the highest attributes that dwell within the human heart.

HOPE ON.

BY ERIC.

THE future seems so dark, O Lord
My feet have grown so weary,
    That sometimes in despondent hours
I feel that I may fail to reach,
The land where light, and joy, and peace]
    Bloom as never-fading flowers.

My heart then trembles with its fear ;
It hardly dares to lift a glance
    Up from the rough, and stony road
On which its dust-stained feet have pressed.
These long, sad, weary toilsome years,
    Bearing its heavy, crushing load.

And yet the distant past recedes,
Its scenes and hills grow dim and faint ;
    Much of the road is journeyed o'er,
Much of the toil has been endured ;
It will not do to languish now,
Push on, my soul and fear no more.

My soul continues marching on,
Through vale, o'er moorland drear and waste ;
    Each day the blest assurance gives
That nearer, nearer is the end
Where full salvation shall be given,
    Where my Redeemer ever lives.

E are satisfied that every intelligent person be lieves, and knows too, that an engagement to marry is a solemn contract between two persons who have plighted their troth to each other. Christian men and women should never fail to first consult the Lord in regard to marrying, as to whether they should accept of such a lady or gentleman to be their husband or wife.

Some people are quick to love on first sight, and hasty about getting married, and often marry without ever knowing or trying to find out anything concerning the principle and general reputation of each other, as to whether she or he would be suitable persons for husband or wife ; to join hearts with in holy wedlock by law for life ; and often the case by not being well enough acquainted with each other. A short time after marriage, trouble enters the family circle, and the first answer is, I am decived. The man, or the woman is not just who I take them to be, but sometimes quick love and hasty marriage almost on the first sight proves true, and the parties live well and enjoy a happy married life. But remember too that it is only throwing away time and money to spend any longer than one year in courtship. All you want is to be well acquainted and make yourselves perfectly satisfied in every respect on both sides, so that when you do make your jump, you may light on the right side. And we believe too that before man and woman shonld enter into holy wedlock for life, under the passion of love, they should carefully consider the matter over, and at the same time seek to know the ways and disposition of each other, in order that neither one will make a mistake.

MY BROKEN-WINGED BIRD.

OR days I have been cherishing
A little bird with broken wing.
I love it in my heart of hearts ;
To win its love I try all arts ;
I call it by each sweet pet name
That I can think its fear to tame.
My room is still and bright and warm ;
The little thing is safe from harm.
If I had left it where it lay
Fluttering in the wint'ry day,
No mate remaining by its side,
Before nightfall it must have died.
It sips the drink, it eats the food ;
Plenty of both all sweet and good.
But all the while my hand it flies,
Looks up at me with piteous eyes ;
From morn till night, restless and swift,
Runs to and fro, and tries to lift
Itself upon its broken wing,
And through the window-pane to spring.

Poor little bird ! . Myself I see,
From morn till night in watching thee.
A Power I can not understand
Is sheltering me with loving hand ;
It calls me by the dearest name,
My love to win, my fear to tame ;
Each day my daily food provides,
And night and day from danger hides
Me safe ; the food, the warmth, I take,
Yet all the while ungrateful make
Restless and piteous complaints,
And strive to break the kind restraints.

REPORT OF BAPTISTS AND METHODISTS OF THE UNITED STATES.

METHODIST EPISCOPAL CHURCH.

Itinerant Ministers, - - - - -	12,507
Local Preachers, - - - - -	12,106
Lay Members, - - - - - -	1,724,420

METHODIST EPISCOPAL CHURCH, SOUTH.

Itinerant Ministers, - - - - -	4,011
Local Preachers, - - - - - -	5,864
Lay Members, - - - - - -	850,811

EVANGELICAL ASSOCIATION CHURCH.

Itinerant Ministers, - - - - -.	926
Local Preachers, - - - - - -	619
Lay Members, - - - - - -	117,027

UNITED BRETHREN CHURCH.

Itinerant Ministers, - - - - - -	2,196
Local Preachers, - - - - - -	———
Lay Members, - - - - - -	157,835

UNION AND AMERICAN CHURCH.

Ministers, - - - - - - -	112
Local Preachers, - - - - - -	40
Lay Members, - - - - - -	3,500

AFRICAN METHODIST EPISCOPAL, ZION CHURCH.

Itinerant Ministers, - - - - -	2,000
Local Preachers, - - - - - -	2,750
Lay Members, - - - - - -	300,000

COLORED METHODIST EPISCOPAL CHURCH.

Itinerant Ministers, - - - - -	638
Local Preachers, - - - - -	683
Lay Members, - - - - - -	125,000

AFRICAN METHODIST EPISCOPAL CHURCH.

Itinerant Ministers,	1,832
Local Preachers,	9,760
Lay Members,	391,044

GRAND TOTAL OF EPISCOPAL METHODISTS IN THE UNITED STATES.

Churches,	17,896
Ministers,	24,222
Local Preachers,	31,823
Members,	3,669,637

A REPORT OF THE NUMBER OF THE BAPTIST DENOMINATION OF THE UNITED STATES, FOR 1883.

REGULAR BAPTIST.

Churches,	24,794
Ministers,	15,401
Members	2,133,044

MISSSONARY BAPTIST.

Churches,	1,090
Ministers,	888
Members,	40,000

FREE WILL BAPTIST..

Churches,	1,485
Ministers,	1,086
Members,	76,706

SEVENTH DAY BAPTIST.

Churches,	87
Ministers,	103
Members,	8,606

SIX PRINCIPAL BAPTIST.

Churches,	20
Ministers,	17
Members,	275

TOTAL NUMBER OF BAPTIST CHURCHES AND MEMBERS OF THE
UNITED STATES.

Churches,	27,476
Ministers,	17,687
Members,	2,258,350

———

GRAND TOTAL OF ALL CHURCHES OF EVERY DENOMINATION OF
THE UNITED STATES, AND TOTAL NUMBER OF ALL
MEMBERS OF SAID CHURCHES OF THE UNION.

Churches,	95,323
Ministers,	. 76,906
Members,	9,982,058

HUSBAND AND WIFE COMBINED.

FTER the marriage of man and woman, according to Scripture, they became one flesh, and are duty bound to work for each others' interest and prosperity. And each one will try to do all in his or her power to keep that vow, which they made in the presence of God and man—to live together in holy wedlock as man and wife—to comfort and cheer each other in sickness and in health, so long as they both shall live. And if either husband or wife does all within his or her power to keep their marriage vow, and at last have to break their vow for protection, they can not be held responsible for the violation of the marriage law upon that one point. For it is intended that every person should protect themselves from harm and danger. (But they both as husband and wife should make up and return, trusting in the Lord, to be united again in union, with more and greater love for each other than they had before, and to avoid the dark clouds of rolling troubles from entering the family circles.) Let the husband and wife be careful to obey, and so manage to treat each other with the greatest of kindness in every respect. They should entertain each other with just as much attention and courtesy as they would a strange lady or a strange gentleman. And another great advantage to the husband and wife is, to keep family troubles forever locked up in their own house. And by observing the above rules they will see the advantage in the coming future. And the husband, who truly loves his wife, and she proves true to him, he will earnestly labor for her comfort, happiness and pleasure in this life. And if a Christian gentleman, he will strive, spiritually, for her joy and everlasting happiness in that better life to come—in Heaven. And the good wife will not fail to do likewise for her husband, which goes to show that true love is that holy passion which God has implanted in the human heart.

And to substantiate all the above facts, which I have written in this book, concerning the duties of the married and the unmarried people, please take your Bibles and turn to the 5th chapter of the book of Ephesians, commencing at the 21st verse and read to the last verse, which will tell the true, binding story of the whole matter. The 28th verse says: "So ought men to love their wives as their own bodies." And the 22nd verse says: "Wives submit yourselves unto your own husbands as unto the Lord."

If hundreds of people, both married and single, young and old, could only be governed by the above rules, which are contained in this book, pertaining to the married subject mainly, there would be no more applications to the courts of the country for divorces—for there would be no more parting of husbands and wives, until death parted them.

And to the unmarried men and women, who are expecting to take to themselves a life-time suiter some day, be slow to speak and quick to think, and give yourselves plenty of time to court and study.

CLOSE OBSERVATIONS.

OON after the first railway was built on Long Island, an old Dutch lady, who had never seen or ridden in a steam-car, told her daughter one bright morning, she thought she would take a ride on the road, just to see how the thing worked.   Accordingly, she went, and after haviug ridden out several miles, returned much pleased with her trip.   In reply to her daughter's inquiry, " Well, mother, what did you see ? " she said, "O nothing much but a haystack, and that was goin' the other way."

Now, my young friends, you are disposed to laugh at this answer of the old lady, but do you know that there are a great many people who travel through this world and never see anything much except haystacks, and they are "going the other way ? "

I am going to talk with you a few moments concerning the importance of cultivating, early in life, the habit of close observation—the habit of noticing things around you with thoughtfulness.

I said, a short time since, to one of my pupils, a young lady who would graduate at the close of the term, who is a good scholar.   " How long have you occupied that room of yours in the boarding-hall ?"

" Nearly three years."

" It has one large window, has it not, with large panes of glass ? "

"How many panes of glass are there in the window ? "
She was surprised that she did not know.

" There are many trees in our school grounds, most de-ciduous, and a very few evergreens.   Among those immediately around the school buildings are the fir or pine more abundant?" I asked ; and again she was surprised to find that she did not know. She will not soon forget the object lesson.

When I first began to teach school in the country, I said to a bright boy, one pleasant spring morning, who had a long mile to come to school every day. " Well, my young man, what did you see this morning on your way to school ? "

" Nothing much, sir."

"I said, "To-morrow morning I shall ask you the same question."

The morning came, and when I called him to my desk, you would have been surprised to hear how much he had seen along the road—cattle of all sizes and colors ; fowls of almost every variety ; sheep and lambs, horses and oxen ; new barns and houses, and old ones ; here a tree blown down, and yonder a fine orchard, just coming out into full bloom ; there a field covered over with corn or wheat ; here a broken rail in the fence ; there a wash-out in the road ; over yonder a pond, alive with garrulous geese and ducks ; here he met a carriage, and there a farm-wagon ; and not only had he seen all these and many more things in the fields, and by the wayside, but looking up had noticed flocks of black-birds going north to their summer home.

GOD IS LOVE.

THE finite mind can not comprehend the full meaning of those three words — "God is love." But it is our privilege, as well as our duty, to study the attributes of God, and the relation in which he stands to his creatures. God is eternal — an uncreated source of wisdom and power, from which flow streams of felicity to gladden the hearts of angels and the inhabitants of the earth.

The grand object which love proposes to accomplish is happiness. All the attributes of God are constantly operating to convince us that he is love, and to prove his matchless love for the happiness of the human family has given the most affecting and impressive display of his true character and will, by sending his well beloved Son into this world. Therefore, we rejoice that God has not left us in the dark, but has given us a divine revelation in which we can acquire a knowledge of his true character and the love he has for the children of men. The apostle says, "Herein is love: not that we loved God, but that he loved us, and sent his Son to be a propitiation for our sins." In this was manifested the love of God toward us, because that God sent his only begotten Son into the world, that we, through him, might live. If God so loved us we ought also to love him.

We are taught in the Scriptures to be imitators of God, and how can we imitate him unless we know something of his true character? If the love of God flows into our hearts we shall know him, for "every one that hath this love is born of God and knoweth God."

The Saviour taught his disciples to be perfect, even as their Father in heaven is perfect, herein is our love made perfect, for we have known and believed the love God hath for us. We may not be able to measure the length and breadth, heighth and depth of God's love, but we can feel and realize that he is love. If we love our enemies, and do good to them who hate us, and pray for them who despitefully use and persecute us, we may be called the children of God; for "he maketh the sun to rise on the evil and on the good, and sendeth the rain on the just and the unjust."

The pure love of God, does not consist of a few transient emotions and fruitless wishes to do others good, but is a substantial and ever-active principle, ready to communicate happiness to every intelligent being. "Love suffereth long and is kind; Love envieth not, vaunteth not itself, doth not behave unseemly, seeketh not her own, is not easily provoked, thinketh no evil." Love worketh no ill to his neighbor. Love is the fulfilling of the law. Dear reader, if we possess this love we may know that we have passed from death to life, for "love is of God, and they that love not knoweth not God, for God is love."

> " Wonderful, wonderful love !
> Wonderful, wonderful love !
> To rescue and save from death and the grave,
> And bring us to heaven above.

UNFAITHFUL SHEPHERDS.

" Take heed therefore unto yourselves and to all the flock.
To feed the church of God which He hath purchased with His
own blood."

H what are the shepherds doing ?
 My sheep are wandering about
With none to look after their goings,
 No one to seek them out.

My sheep are starving and dying,
 On the mountains bleak and bare,
And the tender lambs are crying,
 For food and shelter there.

The wolves have come in amongst them
 And scattered them out in the cold,
And they look to you, oh, ye shepherds,
 To bring them back to the fold.

Arise ! my shepherds ! awaken !
 To the needs of your suffering flock,
And feed them with " bread from Heaven,"
 And with honey " out of the rock."

They have often heard you tell them
 Of a Saviour to save from all sin,
But they've waited long for His coming,
 Still hungry and thirsty within.

Oh lead out your people, my shepherds
 Into the fulness of joy to-day,
The Saviour is willing to bless you,
 Oh hear his sweet call and obey !

Plunge into the fountain of cleansing,
   That washes away every stain,
Accepting the great salvation
   Through faith in the blood of the Lamb.

Be filled with the love of Jesus,
   Receive the anointing within,
Rise up in your power and proclaim Him
   A Saviour *that saves from all sin.*

THE SILENT INFLUENCE

OF NATURE AND OF MAN.

IN these days of advanced civilization, every person is well aware of the fact that the pulpit, the lecture-platform, and the printing press wield over us a mighty influence. Of these we do not now intend to speak, but shall confine our remarks to these silent influences which too frequently escape our notice. How often do we go through life with our senses unobservant! How often do we harden our hearts against the silent voices that would woo us to "the good, the beautiful, and the true!" Yet, the mind awakes to the teachings of silent influence, in the words of the myriad minded Shakespeare, finds "tongues in trees, books in the running brooks, sermons in stones, and good in everything."

To the majority of mankind, there are thousands — nay, millions, of things in this beautiful world of ours, which appear to have been made to no purpose. But have they no mission? Did God really make anything in vain. They speak to us every day ; but not with an audible voice. They enable us to read plainly that, "God is love ;" yet upon their surface we can see neither letters nor words. In the stillness of the midnight hour, when human feet have ceased to tread the earth, if we look out upon the starry heavens, and view those luminous bodies which have stood for ages, and engaged the attention of the best mind, they will exert an influence upon us that will cause man to look up "from nature to nature's God."

How great the truth uttered by David ! "The heavens declare the glory of God, and the firmament showeth his handiwork. Day unto day uttereth speech, and night unto night showeth knowledge." When we consider the moon—that silver queen of night, estimated to be 240,000 miles away— we are apt to think that its mission is only to shed light upon the earth. This is not all it does. For when we think of its magnitude and splendor, we are also led to think of him who made the greater and the lesser lights. Well may the poet beautifully sing :

> "The stars are lighted in the skies,
> Not merely for their shining ;
> But, like the look of loving eyes,
> Have meanings worth divining.
>
> The dew falls nightly, not alone,
> Because the meadows need it,
> But on an errand of its own,
> To human souls that heed it.
>
> Thus nature dwells within our reach,
> But tho' we stand so near her,
> We still interpret half her speech,
> With ears too dull to hear her. "

Whenever we visit an art gallery, and behold some beautiful pictures on exhibition, we are naturally influenced to think of the artist. We seem to have the curiosity to know who painted it—who possessed the genius to portray such a lovely scene on canvas. So, too, is it when we behold the wonderful works of God, the Great artist. The work of a skillful artist is beautiful to look upon ; but it is as nothing when contrasted with the work of God. Generally, the production of an artist is noticed in all its parts at the first or second examination, and ever after appears common to the observer. But not so with the works of God. In all his works we see that which does not appear in art. Every time we look at it, we behold something new, grand, beautiful, and sublime.

"The heavens," in the most emphatic manner, "declare the glory of God." Every star has a voice.

> In reason's ear they all rejoice,
>   And utter forth a glorious voice ;
> Forever singing as they shine,
>   The hand that made us is divine."

Let us now direct our thoughts to some of the silent influences that we find still nearer — influences which are no less powerful in inciting us to deep meditation. Here below, nature, always pleasing, appears with peculiar attraction. What, for instance, is more beautiful to behold than the opening spring, when everything assumes a new and joyous aspect ? A grander and more lovely scene was never presented to the natural eye. Then it is that all nature is joyously arrayed in new and gorgeous apparal. Every mountain, with every volcano, storm, tempest, tree, and flower — *all* show forth the wisdow, power, and goodness of God. Each seems to have a message from the Creator to deliver —a message, not spoken by lips, but which is read upon the very surface of things. The delicate flower that blossoms and blooms in the field, with its exquisite beauty and form, its freshness and its smell, seems to speak to us continually in its silent way, and tells us, "There is a God."

> "Day by day, and hour by hour,
>   As we journey here below,
> Every twig and branch and flower,
>   Tell us they their author know.
>
> What a lesson here is taught us
> Even by a violet blue !
>   God hath made it, yes, to teach us
> We have all some work to do."

If we take a single. leaf from the forest, and compare it with another that seems precisely like it, we shall find that the two are not alike, but entirely different. It is said that God is a "God of vanity." No two things seem to have been made exactly alike by him.

10

Some one, in pointing out the wisdom of God, has said that, "If we take a single drop of water in mid-summer from a pool in an exposed position, and place it under a high magnifying power, while to the naked eye it may appear perfectly clear and pure, yet, under the glass it may appear a grand zoological garden; or, rather, as the Psalmist would say: "a grand and wide sea, wherein are things creeping, innumerable, both small and great beasts." In this miniature sea, as in the great deep, we find animals that feed upon vegetable substances alone, and those also that feed upon other animals; and if we watch their movements for a short time, we shall see an even greater activity than is manifested among higher orders. Thus we see that the microscope brings us into more intimate relation with things immediately about us, opens our eyes to beauties before undreamed of, and, by its mighty yet silent influence, gives us a knowledge of not only the infinity of little things, but also points to a being whose power is unlimited, and whose wisdom is supremely great.

Mr. Spurgeon, the great London preacher, says, "there is a voice in every gale, and a lesson in every grain of dust it bears. Sermons glisten in the morning on every blade of grass, and homilies fly by you as the sere leaves fall from the trees. A forest is a library, a corn-field is a volume of philosophy, the rock is a history, and the river at its base a poem. Go thou who hast thine eyes opened, and find lessons of wisdom everywhere — in the heavens above, in the earth beneath, and in the waters under the earth."

But not only does nature exert a silent, yet powerful influence; man, the noblest work of God, is continually exercising an influence either for good or evil. Every human being, old or young, literate or illiterate, carries with him a moral atmosphere, which is breathed by those he meets and serves to mold their character. The world has never seen the man who could say at the close of his earthly career, that he had not influenced his fellow-creatures in some way — either for good or for evil. As Paul says, "none of us liveth to himself."

The extent of man's influence is incalculable. Not even death destroys it; for it sends its healthful glow across the dark river through the eternal years of our immortality. "It continues to operate after man has mouldered back to dust, and his name has been forgotten. Like the forces of nature, it is often hidden and obscure; but it holds and shakes the world." Well may one say, "the aroma of it fills all the atmosphere; its doctrines distill like the gentle dew; or, like the small rain on the mown grass, its lines go out through all the earth, and its words to the end of the world; there is no speech or language where its speech is not heard." Whatever a man does, or thinks, or feels, even in solitude, has an effect upon the world. For, in the first place, it affects himself and his own character; and that character must influence, in some manner or degree, all with whom he comes in contact.

Every action and look has a voice, and that voice is heard. Deeds are the index of the soul. They proclaim what is within. The eye sees it, and the memory recalls it. Its influence enters the soul and becomes a part of the very being. If it is good, it blesses; if evil, it destroys. Words may be forgotten, but examples never. How often has a look or a gesture left impressions which the flight of years could not efface! A cheerful countenance carries a gleam of sunshine into the darkest alley; while a sad face throws a shadow over those who pass it, even on a crowded thoroughfare. "The impressions which a man thus receives from those with whom he comes in contact, are among the factors which go to make up the aggregate of his own character. That character impinges upon, and helps others; and their's, others; and, so on, for ever. It is impossible for any human being, however wise, to justly estimate the extent and influence of a single individual. Only Omniscience can know how much one good act of an upright man may affect the character and destiny of his fellow creatures.

Now there are many ways in which silent influence is exerted by man. An influence of some kind is exerted by the simple act of walking along the street. We can not look each other into the face without leaving an impression which will influence our future lives to a great degree. "Actions," it is often said, "speak louder than words." And how true! Little do we realize the power — the great power of our actions and our deeds. Their power is felt far and wide nay, their influence reaches from the rivers to the ends of the earth.

Some one has said, "you may build temples of marble, and they will perish; you may erect statues of brass, and they will crumble to dust; but he who works upon the human mind, implanting noble thoughts, and generous impulses, is rearing structures that shall never perish. He is writing upon tablets whose material is indestructible, which age will not efface, but will brighten, and brighten to eternity."

Every day, a mother is exerting an influence upon her child. That influence is for good or evil. She little thinks that, when perhaps she is not saying a word, that child is watching her movements about the house, and being influenced by the very expression which her countenance bears. As the mother is, so the child is apt to be. A very little boy once did wrong, and was sent, after being corrected by his mother, to ask the forgiveness of his heavenly Father.

His offense was passion. Anxious to hear what he would say, his mother followed to the door of his room. In lisping accents she heard him ask to be made better—never to be angry again. And then, with child-like simplicity, he added : "Lord, make ma's temper better too."

" Parents exert a vast amount of influence upon their children without speaking a word. They teach by their example in a most powerful way. They can scarcely do anything which has not an effect upon their children. They may teach well in *words*, but unless they themselves *do* as they teach, it will be of very little use."

Silent influence, we have said, may be exerted in manifold ways. If a gentleman happen to be out on the street late at night, and on his way home, he perchance meets a suspicious character, whom he has every reason to believe intends to rob him, or take his life. The best thing for that man to do as the enemy approaches, is nothing. Let him stand perfectly erect, with his right hand in his bosom, as though he were about to draw therefrom a pistol. His dreaded enemy will then flee from him ; and by this simple act, without uttering a word, he will find that he has saved his life from the hands of a brutal murderer.

All this may seem trivial, strange. But it is a fact, which is constantly being proved in every day life. Not a great while ago, there happened a good illustration of the powerful silent influence in this respect. In the State of Massachusetts, a robber had secreted himself in the chamber of a most respectable and refined lady. The lady, who was without any weapon of defense, was frightened almost to death. What was she to do ? If she attempted to resist in the least, probably it would have cost her her life. And so, without uttering a word, or showing any fear, she went at once to a closet in her room, pretending to get therefrom something in the shape of a pistol.   As luck would have it, she saw what resembled a large pistol, and, approaching the midnight intruder, pointed it at his head.   The man was completely taken by surprise.   He had no thought of a woman exhibiting such boldness.   Thinking his life was in danger, he immediately ran.   The lady followed, all the time pointing the suspected pistol at the man.   We may well imagine the happiness of that lady upon her return to her chamber to rest.

Were we to mention the many like instances in which silent influence has proved a power, this article would swell to a large volume.   Here, there, everywhere its wonderful power is exercised and felt.   We may not always be con scious of its operation ; we may not understand the laws by which it acts; but it goes on, nevertheless, bringing about its astonishing results.   If men, in general, could only realize half the power there is in silent influence—if they, like the brave lady of whom we have just spoken, could always show a fearless and courageous spirit, during such critical times, there would be less occasion for fearing the most outrageous characters who may cross our path.

We have said, man is always exerting an influence upon his fellows either for good or evil.   He *must* exert an influence of some kind.   So long as he lives on the earth—aye, and even after death—he will continue to influence in some way those with whom he was accustomed to associate.   Though dead, yet will he speak.   His words, his deeds, his actions will live.   With a voice, louder (so to speak) than seven peals of thunder, he will still speak to the sons of men, that silent influence, so mysterious in its operation, so sure in effecting its mission, will still go on, and on, and on, helping to mould and shape the life and character of those who yet survive the dead.   Who does not feel that he is influenced largely by the life, (the noble life) of that champion defender of human rights—Charles Sumner? The example of such men lives. Their influence and power are felt throughout the known world. Their memory can never die. "On the record of the grandest movement of the age, culminating in the dominion of right over wrong, in the liberation of millions from thraldom, and in the establishment of freedom over this broad continent, his name will ever stand conspicuous."

"The power of a great life," says George Boutwell, "spreads far beyond the knowledge of names, and is transmitted to generations that have no means of tracing their influence to their source. These influences become woven into the civilization, literature, and politics of nations, control their fortunes, shape their destinies, and work out good or evil results of the most important character."

Can the influence of such men fail to accomplish good in the world? Can their noble deeds for humanity be forgotten? Can they fail to exert an influence for good even though they be numbered with the dead? Never! Their influence must live. It can not die?

Some one has said, "example is the highest moral influence. What we do, will accomplish a hundred fold more than what we say. A good man is a living law to his associates. If he can never speak in public, his example is worth more for truth and virtue than anything he can do by mere exhortation." How true! Many men there are in the world to-day, who are little known by their words and public deeds, but they are doing much good by their example. Their actions speak louder than their words. A good illustration of the truth of this saying, is given in the words of another. He says that "in a certain community, there once lived a man who was an infidel in his sentiments. He was subtile in disposition, and could embarrass most men that encountered him. But there was one man that would never dispute with him. This was a plain, but devoted and consistent christian. His life was a bright focus of vital goodness, and it had more power upon this wicked man than any other sort of artillery that could be brought against him. He was often heard to say that the holy life of this man, was the only thing that gave him trouble. His daily walks had such an influence upon him, that he was finally led to have faith in the reality of the religion of Jesus Christ."

Now, there are hundreds of cases similar to this in which the silent influence of one man has proved a great power for good. The lives of such men are always worthy of imitation. These lives should remind us that,

"We can make our lives sublime.
And departing, leave behind us,
Footprints in the sands of time."

A great many people in this world are influenced, to a great extent, by dreams and midnight visions. If they happen to dream of dying, or meeting with some fearful accident, they will not go out of the house during the whole of the next day, for fear that their dream will come true. Now, while it must be admitted that sometimes dreams do turn out nearly or quite as they were dreamed, there is, nevertheless, no just reason for persons to allow themselves to remain in constant fear, and often neglect the performance of their daily duties. People, as a rule, are too superstitious in these days. They can be influenced more or less by any fancy of the mind. If they see anything white at night, in the form of man, they declare it is nothing less than a ghost.

On the south coast of England, many years ago, there lived a widowed lady, and her children in a very large, old-fashioned house. She had many servants, and every luxury that wealth could give. But, unfortunately, she had no neighbors. The nearest village was some distance off. The house in which the family lived, had once been a castle. Long corridors led to apartments that were seldom, if ever used. It happened once that a person was sick in one of these distant rooms, and a nurse, in attendance upon the sick, was much frightened at seeing the head of one of the old portraits on the wall move as though there were life in the portrait. She said she was certain that the eyes winked, and the head moved. At the first opportunity she ran off to tell her mistress. Sometime after this circumstance, the oldest son returned home from the army. A soldier is always bold; and, hearing about the matter, he resolved to sleep in the room and see if there were really any marvelous appearances. His mother and sister tried in vain to keep him from sleeping in the haunted chamber. He persisted. The family retired, and he was left alone. The next morning he appeared looking very pale, and refused to say whether he saw anything or not.

In about a week after, the young man told his mother that they must all leave the house. They moved. The old habitation was pulled down, and it became known that a cave situated under the said haunted chamber, was used by smugglers who wished to frighten the family from occupying the rooms over the cave. One of the smugglers had cut a hole through a partition between the chamber and a dressing room, and made the opening just behind a large portrait. It seems he had moved the painting from the frame thereof, and put himself in its place. This he did to frighten the family, and make them believe the chamber was haunted.

Thus we see how great an influence may be exerted upon some people by so simple an occurrence. It takes very little to excite some individuals.

It is impossible for us, in this paper, to show the many ways in which silent influence is so powerfully exerted. Time would fail us were we to speak of the influence of christianity and religion, of light and darkness, of heat and cold, and a thousand other things which serve to benefit and bless the world. All around us are influences which seem to have a voice that speaks of the power and wisdom of God. Byron well says:

> There's music in the sighing of a reed,
> There's music in the gushing of a rill;
> There's music in all things, if men had ears;
> There earth is but an echo of the spheres."

There is one other example of the power of silent influence to which we must allude ; and that is conscience. What a powerful influence is exerted by conscience! The work it does is done quietly, and silently ; but it is done nevertheless, and done well. A good illustration of the influence of conscience is here given.

"An old Indian asked a white man to give him some tobacco for his pipe. The man gave him a loose handful from his pocket. The next day he came back and asked for the white man; "For said he, I found a quarter of a dollar among the tobacco."

" Why, don't you keep it ?" asked a bystander.

" I've got a good man and a bad man here," said the Indian, pointing to his breast; and the good man say, 'it is not mine, give it back to the owner.' The bad man say ; 'Never mind; you have got it, and it is your own.' The good man say, ' no, no, you must not keep it. So I don't know what to do, and I think to go to sleep, but the good and the bad man keep talking all night, and trouble me ; and now I bring the money back, I feel good."

Like the old Indian, we have all a good and a bad man within. The bad man is temptation ; the good man is conscience.

In conclusion, let us remember that each of us has the power to exert an untold influence for good. Let us use that influence. Let us use it for the good of humanity. In our moral nature there is a chord of sympathy which seems to vibrate from heart to heart. Our emotions may be transmitted, in some cases, by the voice and by the pen. Let us use, then, the voice, the pen, the heart—yea, the whole being, for the welfare of those in the midst of whom we live.

GRANTED WISHES.

TWO little girls let loose from school
 Queried what each would be.
One said, " I'd be a queen and rule ; "
 And one, "the world I'd see."

The years went on. Again they met
 And queried what had been ;
" A poor man's wife, am I, and yet,"
 Said one, " I am a queen.

" My realm a happy household is,
 My king a husband true ;
I rule by loving services ;
 How has it been with you ? "

One answered, " Still the great world lies
 Beyond me as it laid ;
O'er love's and duty's boundaries
 My feet have never strayed.

" Faint murmurs of the wide world come
 Unheeded to my ear ;
My widowed mother's sick bedroom
 Sufficeth for my sphere."

They clasped each other's hands ; with tears
 Of solemn joy they cried,
God gave the wish of our young years,
 And we are satisfied."

THE DAY LABORER.

MONG the distinct statements concerning the econo-mies which God has instituted, we find this verse of scripture : "Man goeth forth unto his work, and to his labor, until the evening." It teaches that the Creator's plan of worlds, implies human industry. The word man, here, is general ; it includes all men, and all women—the aggregate of humanity ; it associates labor with every individual of the race. Daily work is announced as a settled fact, in the arrangement of nature, and sung as a pæan of praise to the Lord. The will of heaven toward men is that they should have regular employment. Labor is as necessary and as dignified as the revolving of the sun, in his circuit, the changing of the moon, the harvest yield of the earth, the coursing of the waters down the valleys, and among the hills, the distribution of the rain, the sweep of the tides, or any other of the movements of inanimate crea-tion. The Psalmist puts all celestial and terrestial opera-itons in sublime accord with the every day duties of men. It is so much the divine will and plan that human hands should be busy, as it is that nature should observe her ap-pointments from the beginning until the end of time. Every created finger has its place and its work, and is, in its errands, as important in the grand running of things, as any star that shines, or any world that yields its increase.

The Bible makes human labor a sacred ordinance, and claims a special service from every hand, as well as from every head and every heart. The gift of reason includes the obligation to work. Man's physical existence is de-pendent on the use of his own hands. His food and raiment are to be wrought out of crude elements by toil, tact, and patience. The beasts have matured provision for all their wants. They are fed and clothed by the hand that created, and have ample and reasonable supplies. But man must coax the earth for his bread ; he draws his comforts from reluctant sources. He must build his own shelter, weave his own garments, invent and provide his own accommodations. Nature is a storehouse of ready made wares, free and full, for brute and bird, for fish and fowl, for insect and reptile, all the year and every where ; but man must look for himself. He is furnished with raw materials only. He must work them into supplies, or shiver and starve. Nature gives to man but hints and helps. She hides her gold deep in the mountains, her pearls deep in the sea, and says: "Now dig and dive, and you shall have them." She puts her bearded wheat and delicious fruits forward of the seedtime, and the planting by tedious months and years, with storm and snow between; and the sower, and the planter must wait, watching and tilling the ground until the gleaning days. Dwellings are to be delved out of the quarries, cut out of the forests ; clothes are to be spun from the wool the cotton, and the flax, and woven in the loom ; all essentials, and all luxuries are alike to be reached only by search and struggle and sweat ; and no era shall ever dawn to change this divinely appointed method of living by labor; day by day, and century by century, while the world endures.

"No man is born into the world whose work
Is not born with him ; there is always work,
And tools to work withal, for those who will ;
And blessed are the horny hands of toil."

REHOBOAM.

EHOBOAM was a man whose opportunies for usefulness were very great. He was the son of Solomon,
and his successor to the throne of Israel. Possessing
high social position, and mental culture, with abound-
ing wealth, he might have been a blessing instead of a curse
to his people. He seemed wanting in the true elements of
greatness, Christian integrity, with a fixedness of purpose,
and a strict adherence to principle. Solomon, his father,
when ascending the throne asked for wisdom that he might
wisely rule so great a people. A prayer hearing God not
only gave him his desire, but added "riches, and wealth,
and honor" above the kings of earth. We are not impressed, however, with the belief that his course of life was
calculated to impress the mind of his son with a high sense
of christian obligation and duty.

Solomon had heavily taxed the people to erect the temple
on Moriah, and other costly and magnificent buildings ; and
they thought their burdens should be lessened when the
necessity for their continuance ceased. They sent a dele-
gation to Rehoboam stating their willingness to serve him,
provided he would accord to them their rights as subjects.
Instead of profiting by the counsel of older and experienced
heads around him, he listened to the advice of younger ones,
as ignorant of the rights and feelings of the people as he was.
Hence the disastrous results that followed. Some of the
tribes, despairing of equity and justice under his rule, re-
nounced their fealty to his rule, and declared they had no
"inheritance in the son of Jesse." Solomon, the builder

of the temple, had passed away, and Rehoboam, his successor, by his imprudence, had severed the connecting links
that bound the tribes together in the pride and in the bonds
of a common brotherhood.   Shishak, king of Egypt, seeing
the impotency of a dismembered, scattered, and ruined people, came up against Jerusalem, and stripped the temple,
and the richly furnished palaces of David's son of their dec-
orations and their treasures.   Instead of learning wisdom
from those capable of imparting it, that he might clearly
see and perform his duty to his God and his country, he pursued a course of policy that brought ruin upon his head, nor
awake to the perils of the situation, until he saw the fearful
"Ichabod" inscribed upon his throne.   In his humiliation
he saw the shades of thickening darkness gathering around his
throne, and its waning glory departing.   He saw the magnificent temple that crowned the summit of Moriah, which
his father had built, decorated and adorned, despoiled of its
beauty, and its treasures snatched away by Egypt's king.
He saw the ivory throne on which his father sat, in the days
of his transcendent glory and power, with its twelve golden
lions, emblems of power and might, undermined and up-
rooted by the sacriligious hands of an invader in search of
gold.   He saw the richly decorated halls of his father's pal-
ace, where once he sported in the thoughtless innocency of
his childhood days, with the dazzling splendor that adorned
them in the reign of David's son, lonely, desolated and
ruined.   What feelings of sadness must have pressed his
burdened soul as memory recalled the scenes of the past,
when Sheba's queen admired the grandeur, glory and power
of the realm, and songs of triumph floated out o'er Shiloh's
streams.

David was a king the people delighted to honor.   And
the wisdom of Solomon, and the dazzling of his throne at-

tracted the envy and gaze of less fortunate rulers of earth. But Rehoboam, instead of improving his time, his talents, and his treasure, in promoting the harmony and prosperity of his people, drove them to desperation by a disregard of their wishes and their interests. Standing, as it were, upon a volcano whose smouldering fires were gathering in their intensity, ready to burst forth in resistless fury at his feet, he saw not the deep feelings of discontent that pervaded the minds of his subjects until the thunders of a fearful disintegration aroused him to the perils of his condition. But alas! it was too late to repair the evils of his heedless and misguided course. The cry had gone up, "every man to your tents, O Israel." The opportunity for arresting the tide of discontent had passed, and the goodly heritage of his fathers felt the scourge of an invading foe. Had Rehoboam sought counsel from wiser heads, instead of listening to boys around him, a brighter day might have dawned upon his reign. But, like too many sons of fortune in our land, whose prudent fathers secured for them a competence, his prospects for happiness and usefulness were blighted by pursuing an illadvised course. Failing to appreciate the duties of his high position, and secure the esteem and respect of others around him, he reaped the bitter fruits of his folly. He saw the morning sun of his glory, that rose so brightly, setting in a thickening cloud of discontent, the accumulated treasures of his father departing, and the soil of Israel pressed by an insulting and a plundering foe. With an united Israel, attached to their king and their country, the footprints of Egypt's king would not have desecrated her temple and her soil.

The course pursued by Solomon's son in rejecting the counsel of the sages of the land, reminds us so much of the course pursued by some sons of fortune in our midst, whose sun goes down in moral darkness, and pecuniary ruin.

11

Prudent and economical parents toil to give their boys a good education, and accumulate riches for them, that they may occupy a position of usefulness and respectability in society.   But how few are fully aware of the heartfelt solicitude and anxiety of a father's heart for their present and future welfare.   Their parents carry them to the house of God when young, invoke the blessings of heaven upon them, and pass away, leaving them the inheritors of their hard-earned treasures.   Flatterers cajole and deceive them— congenial spirits gather around them, and with the remembrance of a pious father's example fading from their mind, they run farther and farther in sin until designing "Shishak's" strip them of their means, leaving them in pennyless poverty and degredation.   Like the prodigal they find themselves in wretchedness and in want, either the associates of the swine or viler sons of men.

Young man, you are to be the representative of your family when the silvery locks of your time-honored father, will be seen no more in time.   Lift up your head, and "shew thyself a man."   Stand up in the upright integrity of a noble and a generous nature, and let the impulses of a manly dignity of character move thee to action.   Let the sunlight of a pure and a spotless life elevate the thoughts and affections of thy heart, and shed a brighter luster in the moral atmosphere above the father's grave.   "Wisdom was given to direct."   Hence says the wise man—"Get wisdom, and with all thy getting get understanding."   "Wisdom is the principal thing—she shall bring thee to heaven, when thou do'st embrace her."   Young man your parents love you. They will soon be gone.   Respect their feelings and gladden their hearts by a thoughtful course of action.   Remember the words of the wise man—"A wise son maketh a glad father; but a foolish son is the heaviness of his mother."

THE LITTLE GIRLS' PRAYER-MEETING.

KITTY was a romping, noisy, quick-tempered, impulsive child; but though she often tore her clothes, and broke dishes, and made trouble for her mother, she tried hard to be good, and used to pray every night and morning, asking God to forgive her sins, and make her a good girl. When she was seven years old a minister moved into the neighborhood, and his little Nellie and Kittie soon became fast friends. Every day they went to the same school, and played together, and each soon learned that the other prayed and was trying to be good. One morning, Kitty came bounding into the minister's house, shouting, "O Nellie! Can't you "—when she saw a sight that stopped her feet and tongue, and brought a solemn hush upon her soul. The minister, his wife, and all the children, Nellie among them, were kneeling before their chairs, and some one was praying aloud. Kitty had never seen a family at prayer before, and she went out very softly. After that she used to watch Nellie while playing, and think, " I wish *we* had prayers like Nellie's folks."

One day during vacation, they were playing together, when Kitty suddenly stopped and asked, "Do *you* pray in the morning, when your father does?"

"Yes. Don't you?" said Nellie.

"My folks never pray," said Kitty. "Oh, dear! I wish they did. It would help me so much to be good if anybody prayed with me. I get lonesome trying all alone."

"I'll pray with you," said Nellie. " Can't we have a little prayer-meeting all by ourselves?"

"Oh, yes," cried Kitty, joyfully. "Let's go where no-body can see us, and have one now."

"Where can we go ?" said Nellie. "Oh, I know; down by the thornbush back of the shed."

So, with their arms around each other, the two little girls went to that shady retreat hidden out of sight from the road and houses, and kneeling down together, asked the good Lord to wash away their sins for Jesus sake, and help them to be good children while at work or at play. After they had prayed, a deep peace came into their hearts, and kissing each other, they parted and went to their homes — Kitty wondering at the quiet joy in her heart, and breaking into little snatches of song as she helped her mother about get-ting dinner.

· "Can't we have a prayer-meeting every day?" was the first thing Kitty said the next time they met.

"I want to," said Nellie. "What time can we meet?" "I can't come very early," said Kitty, for I have to wash dishes and sew a 'stint' on patchwork every forenoon; but I get through by ten o'clock, generally, if I am smart. When I cry and make a fuss I don't get through so quick."

"Let's have it at eleven, then," said Nellie.

"And let's invite Annie to come, too," said Kitty. "She prays when she goes to bed. I know, 'cos I've slept with her."

So after that, every fair day while vacation lasted, the lit-tle girls met at eleven o'clock, and prayed together. Some-times they sang a hymn, and sometimes Nellie would tell the others what her father or mother had said about Jesus, and the different ways she could please Him. And these little meettngs helped the children to "grow in grace, and in the knowledge of the Lord and Saviour, Jesus Christ."

I WILL NEVER LEAVE YOU.

THERE is only one who can say this. Every human tie is liable to be severed, nor can we assure ourselves of the permanence of any earthly friendship. Those nearest and dearest to us may turn to be our bitterest foes; and those whose friendship remains unbroken may yet be swept away from our presence and fellowship, and leave us desolate and alone. But "He hath said I will never leave you nor forsake you." The seal of truth is upon the covenant which He hath made with us. Long as His blood avails; long as His grace abides; long as His mercy endures, long as His omnipotence rules, and His omniscience discerns; long as creation is subject to its Maker's sway; long as the stormy wind fulfills His word; long as the thunderbolts sleep within His hand; long as the angels wait to do His will, hearkening to the voice of his command; so long we need not fear; so long we shall not be abandoned, for He hath said, "I will never leave you nor forsake you."

The sun may grow dim in the heavens; the stars may burn out in the distant sky; heaven and earth may pass away; the sea may vanish from our view; men may fall from their steadfastness, and angels may fail to keep their high estate, but the Lord's promise will not fail, and He will fulfill all His word. With this assurance we may bid adieu to anxiety and fear, and heed that word which says, "Let your conversation be without covetousness, and be content with such things as ye have, for He hath said, I will never leave you nor forsake you. So that we may boldly say, the Lord is my helper, I will not fear what man shall do unto me."

RELIGION is a life. It is a life of good deeds. A man's faith or profession is vain unless there is right living. A life of piety toward God, and of charity toward men is the only true life. Such a life comprehends faithfuluess to all our obligations, which are summed up as follows: "Thou shall love the Lord thy God with all thy heart, and thy neighbor as thyself." This is right living. This is religion as viewed from a christian standpoint.

The Bible furnishes us with a portraiture of the life that is well pleasing to God. It is a pure and blameless life. Zacharias and Elizabeth present to us an example of right living. "They were both righteous before God, walking in all the commandments and ordinances of the Lord blame- less." It is not enough to have faith or emotions. They are important, but only as they are connected with a good life. The life is more than feeling or sentiment, or any such thing. It is true, however, that the faith, feelings, senti ments and purposes of the heart make the life, and that all these things enter largely into the formation of character. And then character determines the life, and character de- termines the destiny of every man. "We must stand before the judgment seat of Christ, that every one may receive the things done in his body according to that he hath done, whether it be good or bad." By the principals of right liv- ing, every one must stand or fall in the great day. God is good; He is merciful, and will save all who live godly in Christ Jesus. All who fear God and work righteousness are accepted by Him. Blessed life!

THE GOOD OF KNOWLEDGE.

BY A PUBLIC ORATOR.

THE household god next in importance, and which is perhaps the most popular both of the household and the nation, is the god of education falsely so-called. Everything must bow to the scholastic education of the children. Their very health is sacrificed in hundreds of instances; the whole of the domestic arrangements, the convenience of father and mother, and visitors must bow down to this god. The children must be educated whatever else becomes of them. I touched very briefly on this subject in my address at Exeter Hall on "Family Religion," and some friends seem to infer that I was against education, whereas I have seldom talked with anyone on the subject more profoundly impressed with its importance ! I adopted many years ago the sentiment of that great philosopher Locke, who said that " in nine cases out of ten all the men we meet are what they are for good or for evil, for usefulness or otherwise, by their education." I say I fully believe that, and have acted upon it in training my own family, so you see my quarrel is not with education, but with a certain kind of education.

I believe that a child ought to be educated every half-hour of its life—never ought to be left to itself in the sense of not having a recognized influence exerted over its mind. The question is then, what *kind* of education is the right kind to bestow upon children ? How ought you to educate them ? The same idea which helped us on the question of fashion, may help us again here. What should be the great

purpose of education?   Surely right education must be that
which is calculated to help the child to attain the highest
type of its kind, and to fit it for its highest destiny.   You train
your horses on that principle.   You develope and strengthen
it that it may be a perfect creature, having capacity devel-
oped for the highest service of which its nature is capable.
I say that all right training ought to contemplate this end,
especially so with respect to man, being God's highest creature.   Next comes the question, what *is* the highest type
of a man ? and the highest destiny of a man ?   That is the
point.   What ought we to aim at ?   For if the aim is wrong,
all our training will be wrong.   I say that the highest type
of a man is that in which the *soul* rules over the body, in
which a purified, ennobled soul rules through an enlightened
intelligence, and makes every faculty of the being subserv-
ient to the highest purpose, the service of humanity, and
the service of God !   If I understand it, that is the highest
type of man and his highest destiny.   And it seems to me
that all education that falls short of this is a curse rather
than a blessing.

The aim of all rightly directed education is to make such
men and women and to fit them for such work, and if it
fails of this, I say it is one sided, unphilosophical and irre-
ligious, and that is my quarrel with modern education.   I
charge it with being all this, and that is the reason I did not
educate my children after its theories.   I did not believe in
them, and the results so far prove that I was right.

Then first let us look at what ought to be the purpose of
education.   Most of you, nearly all I presume, agree as to
what I have stated.   But the purpose of modern education
is anything but this.   It is for the most part planned and
executed with a view to aggrandizement or well-being of
the individual looked at in a worldly point of view.

Parents look at their boy and say, "Now what can we do with him?" They have all sorts of aspirations and ambitions for the boy, and they feel, "Well, we must educate him, develope his intellect"—what for? That he may use it for the service of humanity and the glory of God? Oh no, that never enters their minds. They say, "We will have him educated in order that he may shine in the world, or get up in the world. We will have a son that will be able to go to the bar, the senate house," or do anything else that their ambition fixes on. The aggrandizement of the individual is the end, not the universal good, and out of this wrong aim arises the undue estimate of mere scholastic education. What would you say of the trainer of an animal, if it were possible for the trainer to select one faculty, and develop and strengthen that, to the exclusion, neglect, or extinction of other faculties, would you say that was right training?

The main idea of modern education is that of the imparting of knowledge. Knowledge is the idol which both the household and the nation to-day are worshipping more largely perhaps than any other, as if progress in knowledge constituted the true progress of man. Oh, if it were so what a different world we should have to-day ; but we know it is quite the contrary. We know that the more knowledge you give to an individual without giving him a corresponding disposition to use it for good, the more you increase his capacity for mischief. Very often the most learned men live for the worst purposes! But, alas! the very flower of the youth of our nation are sacrificed to this modern deity. The notion is that our youth must be educated in this mischievious sense, they must be crammed with knowledge. Whether it be a curse or a blessing to them is not the question! *they must have it.* They must learn the dead languages, and they must read bad literature in order to make them like the rest of the world around them.   No matter what becomes of their morals, they must be crammed with science, much of it falsely so-called; much of it in embryo, crude and shallow—the shallow theories of minds trying to grasp profound thoughts, and getting lost in the fogs of their own folly, and landing the poor pupils on the strand of infidelity and atheism.   The intellect, the one faculty of the man, must be strained, and stretched, and crammed to the utter neglect, and often destruction, of the moral faculties; and when you have done that, what have you produced? — an enlightened animal, an intellectual monster, who walks abroad, treading under his feet all the tender instincts and most sacred feelings and aspirations of humanity.   That is all you have produced; there they are, thousands of such to be seen to-day.   Alas! my heart bleeds over the stories I hear all over the land, which I could give you as illustrations of this fact.   All this mischief comes of upsetting God's order—cultivating the intellect at the expense of the heart; being at more pains to make your youth *clever* than to make them good?   This false theory leads to false methods, and hence the deplorable condition of our nation to day.   It leads to the separating from home life our little boys of ten and twelve years of age, and our girls too, alas! sending them away from the tender influences, and what ought to be the grand and noble inspirations of their mothers, to herd with boys of their own age and class, and to have their moral nature manipulated by masters, often skeptical or immoral instead of their own mothers.   Now I can say and will maintain, that the chief end of education is not mere teaching but inspiration, and if you fail to inspire your pupil with nobleness, disinterested goodness, truth, morality, and religion, not only are all the glorious ends of education lost, but you damn your pupil more deeply than he might have been damned without your education. I ask, is it not so? Take some of your own sons, alas! (and I could point to numbers round about) as illustrations of this fact. God has given every child a tutor in his mother, and she is the best and only right tutor for the heart.

I defy you to fill a mother's place for influence over the heart. If God were to depute the angel Gabriel, he could not fill the mother's place. God has tied the child to its mother by such peculiar moral and mental links that no other being could possibly possess. And I tell you mothers here that if you are good mothers you are committing the greatest wrong to send away your child from your homes, and I believe this is damning half our nation to-day. God, you see, committed the child to its parents to be educated, not to the schoolmaster. You can employ the schoolmaster to teach his head, and even then you must be very careful what sort of a schoolmaster he is, or he will ruin the child. But God committed him to the parents to be educated, trained, that is, taught how to *feel*, *think*, and *act* not to the schoolmaster. And it is to the mother especially that belongs the art and the capacity to inspire her boy to love all that is noble and good, and disinterested, and grand in humanity, and keep on inspiring him until he is strong enough in moral excellence; in other words, strong enough in God's likeness to walk alone. Just as you tend him when he is a baby, and will not leave him to strangers to train him to walk and speak, so while he is a moral infant you are to watch and keep and train him until he is able to walk alone. I set my soul on this with regard to my own children, and God has enabled me to do it. I had a great fight over it in many ways, but I said : "I am *determined* to keep my children for God and goodness.   They shall have the education that I think likely to help them to be useful to their generation, as far as possible ; but I never will sacrifice purity to polish, I will never sacrifice the heart to the head." That was my resolve, and I see no cause to regret it.

HOPE.

ID it ever occur to you what a world of thought is wrapped up in that little word "hope?" Its very pronunciation makes every bosom bound and burn. It is music to the ear of the young, health to the sick, and life rejuvenated to the old. Poetry makes hope a formation, grief makes it a solace, and desolation makes it the brightest flower that adorns earthly creation, while even disappointment and delusion whisper darkness out of the sky of to-day, into sunshine of to-morrow. Sobbing sorrow may crush and cripple the soul, but hope gives it new elasticity. Nay, it may be humiliation in the dust, but hope will raise it up again. Hope is man's birthright, which, after all his blandishments, delusions, and mockeries, never maketh him ashamed to hope on, hope ever. Airy fancies may allure him, and smiling faces beguile him into treachery, but hope fits etertnal around the human head and breast, and hangs the rainbow on the blackest cloud in all the chaste sparklings of an angel from immortal life. Thunder-bolts may leap from the fair bow in the clouds, and hope may vanish as a fair scorner from that bright spot, but the fascinating form soon appears elsewhere in fairer robes than ever, and with a wreath of flowers, to crown the child of endless disappointments. Now when you connect the word "hope" with "salvation," then what a wonderful word it becomes! At once it comes to measure man's most delightful Christian attainment. Indeed, so intimately is it associated with practical godliness, that religion itself is called "a good hope through grace.". More than this, our God is called the God of hope, our Saviour is called Christ, our hope, and his finished work is known as "the hope set before us in the gospel," while those who accept him are said, "to rejoice in the hope of the glory of God."

THE BRICKLAYER.

BY ALEXANDER CLARK.

THE tents of the moving masses had hitherto been their most substantial dwellings ; but now there is to be marked an era of change in the material of their habitations. The transient and flimsy fabric of pole and canvas is to give place to buildings with fixed foundations. Wandering tribes are about to assume permanent abodes, and to establish citizenship, and civil relations.

The family now recognize the community ; society takes its place in the economy of Providence. The land of Shinar, on the rich plains that bordered the Euphrates, was beautiful and luxurious, but destitute of stone ; and its soil yielded no lime for cement, and hence, in the early history of architecture, there arose a necessity for invention. The sandy clay was found to be easily moulded, and sunburnt into convenient forms that would answer in the place of stones ; and a kind of bitumen or slime which floated on the ponds and marshes, was substituted for mortar to bind the bricks into solid walls.

It was here, of such materials, and by men theretofore of one language, that the tower of Babel was attempted, as a refuge against another flood. The people were not willing to trust God's word, though stamped with the rainbow seal, that there should be no more deluge, but rather inclined to believe in brick of their own hands' making, than in the promise of the almighty.

Cities and towers from this time forward began to dot the post diluvian world. The manufacture and laying of bricks were the occupations of multitudes of busy men. There are still in existence in Egypt both public and private buildings erected with the kind of materials described by Moses in the Pentateuch. The Babylonian bricks were about one foot square, and three and a half inches thick. They bore various inscriptions and patterns on their surface, cast in their moulding. Really the art of printing might be said to date its origin in this custom. Old bricks have been discovered at Nineveh and Thebes bearing the ovals of a king, and the names and offices of the priests.

Both sun dried and kiln-burnt bricks were common in the treasure cities and granaries of lower Egypt. The clay from the banks of the Nile was carried in baskets, thrown into mass, saturated, and trodden into the proper temper by the feet of the workmen. It was a most fatiguing and perilous toil. Nahum refers to the severity of such service in his prophecy, III chapter, and 14th verse. " Draw the waters for the siege, fortify thy strongholds ; go into clay, and tread the mortar, make strong the brickkiln." Wherever there was any difficulty in procuring desirable stones. the Romans, in later ages, resorted to the use of bricks. The Roman bricks were from eighteen to thirty inches in length, nine inches in width, and two and three-fifths inches in thickness, and originated a style of architecture peculiar to their shape. Bricks were less used during the early part of the middle ages ; but about the twelfth century were generally employed in Northern Italy, and in the adjacent provinces. By the sixteenth century, brick almost superceded stone, and many of the great cathedrals and prominent public works of engineering were executed of bricks even where stone was accessible. In later years the taste is changing again, and stone work comes to the front in fashionable architecture, and bricks are pressed into rear walls and unpretending structures.

The various colored bricks, red, yellow, blue, and brown are obtained from clays of peculiar tints. The east Pennsylvania pressed bricks have a brilliant red appearance, while the common and scarcely less beautiful bricks of Wisconsin, are cream tinged, and in those cities the walls hold their primitive colors ; while in Pittsburgh, Wheeling, and other places, whatever may have been the original hue of houses, they soon became shadowed with the smoke and soot of the bituminous fires. And so does many a man's religion, however bright and clear at first, sometimes become tinged with the prevailing atmospheres. It were well, however, if the shade on men gets no thicker than on houses. There are solid bricks, red and clean at heart, in the walls of the dimmest old church, under the settling smoke. So be it evermore, beyond our sight with the varied human portions that compose the temple of the living God, though oft obscured without, and dull with the dust and grime of business—may they be pure and clean within.

THE HELPER HELPED.

———

THE above truth is very clearly expressed in the proverb—" He that watereth shall be watered also himself." This is very simple language, and yet in what simple language almost all the great truths of God are expressed. So simple are some of the facts that we fear on that account they are overlooked. It is the case frequently that in our rambles through the fields we crush or trample upon a flower because it is not large or showy, and yet if we were to take it in our hands and examine it, we would discover that it was not so simple after all. It is the same with men who carelessly or listlessly go through the scriptures, some great truths are overlooked or despised, simply because they are not expressed in high sounding words and phrases.

We like truths expressed in simple language, they are none the less effective because of their simple attire, as the violet is none the less sweet because of its modest bearing. It is so with the truth with which we started out, it is simple in language, and yet it expresses to us the great truth of man's relation to his fellow man, and his influence upon him. The whole universe is so closely related that one part affects the other, as men influence for good or for evil their fellowmen. But do we know this truth rightly? Has it been brought home to our hearts by experience? It is evident that we do not understand this language or we would carry it out in our dealings with the world. There is a reflex power in doing good. A good action will act upon the doer. We seek to do ourselves all the good we can, and yet we ignore the way by which God has designed we should be blessed. This fact leads us to think that we do not rightly see the force of the truth expressed in this proverb.

We see a man faltering and sinking under a heavy weight, it may be that he is poor and aged, and that the load upon his shoulders is either to feed or warm those who are dependent upon him. We help to carry his burden. His heart is made glad and thankful. The exercise has made us stronger in body, and the kind intent has made us happier in soul. You see another going the downward way to ruin. You take it upon yourself to rescue him, the effort you make on his behalf only makes you the firmer. Another is withering under the blighting influence of some sin. You bring to that soul the water of life, and that very action brings upon your own soul the dew of heaven.

See how the law of God acts even in nature. The earth gives its vapors to the sky, and these come back again in the form of rain to refresh the earth. The trees draw nutriment from the soil, then shed their leaves which in return enrich the soil. It is so with our good actions, we send them out, and they come back to us like the bread upon the water. What blessings we may be the means of scattering far and wide. How we have it in our power to carry into the recesses of our souls sunshine and gladness by making the atmosphere around others more congenial. We do not appreciate as we should the privilege we have of being helpers. We are shrewd enough in drawing from our fellowmen that which will add to our wealth, but that which brings us peace of conscience, and happiness, we are not so apt to receive because we do not give. How many souls there are to be helped and watered, and what are we doing as the instruments of God? Opportunities are thick about us, and our hands must not rest. In sowing we shall also reap. It is

a law of God, that every good deed performed will bring the
doer a harvest in some way or other.   We have experienced
this time and again in various ways.   Who has not been repaid by watering withered flowers.   Who has not been rec-
ompensed a thousand times over by watering withering
souls.   Who has not received ten-fold in doing the kind act.
Just call up a circumstance.   You sat in your own comfortable home, with abundance about you—a knock at the door
calls you.   There stands a poor child shivering in the cold,
begging for help.   You knew the family, and knew they
needed help.   You gave liberally.   As you turned back to
your own warm fireside, and thought of the brightened
countenance of that child, and of the joy your help would
bring the family were you not repaid?   Did not that act done
in the spirit of the Master bring to your own heart such a joy
as can not be described?   "Inasmuch as ye did it unto one
of the least of these, ye did it unto me."   Do good and you
will get good.   It is only by sowing that you can hope to
reap.

KITCHEN GARDEN.

BY LUCIA E. F. KIMBALL.

BOUT six weeks before Thanksgiving day, there came to one of our homes, a forlorn, wretched women—girl she might have been called, for she was only twenty, and that score of years had brought her nothing of womanhood's royal estate. She was a pitiful sight, without any bonnet, and with scarcely clothing enough to cover her. Haggard and hungry and wild looking, she seemed a blot on God's fair universe. The bleared eyes peered in at the basement window, and met those of a loving, christian woman, who pitied her condition, and bid her welcome to come in, knowing her to be one whom Christ died for, and in this home she found shelter, comforts and patient instruction. And with much pains taken, she was very soon taught to cook and do general house work, of which she was almost wholly ignorant. She was very apt after recovering from a low state of degredation, to learn how to carry on business about the house. A new world seemed to have opened on this poor girl, and again, and again she would speak out in high words of gratitude. O, Mrs. G. how much better it would have been if you had only taken me in years ago, and learned me how to work. So she thanks the Lord for the good missionary. Just see how such wrecking of humanity can be prevented. Gladly we turn on it the calcium light of a beautiful charity, which aims to save girls from such a hapless fate, in so much as idleness, and contempt for labor are fruitful causes of ruined lives.

A school not unlike the kindergarten. The same bright, airy rooms. The same kind, inspiring teaching, but the playthings are toy kitchen utensils and household furniture. Here the children are taught to work in such an attractive and fascinating way that naturally they come to love it. The lessons are set to pretty songs, accompanied by exercises and plays. We give a few :

Washing dishes, that Gibralter of housework. A pretty toy dish-pan is placed before each little housemaid, and she plays wash the dishes, rinsing them in clear water, and drying each article on its special towel, while to the piano they sing :

> Washing dishes,
>   Suds are hot,
> Work away briskly,
>   Do not stop.
>
> First the glasses ;
>   Wash them well ;
> If you do them nicely,
>   All can tell.
>
> Then the silver
>   Must be bright, etc.,

. When we remember how much there is in the "feel" of a drinking-glass, we are glad to know that the children "are taught to not only wipe a glass on the glass-towel, but also to set it down with the towel, without touching it with the hands."

For bed-making each child is furnished with a doll's bedstead, with regular bedding. The clothes are carefully removed and laid over small chairs; pillow-shams folded ; the mattress thoroughly shaken ; then the bed smoothly and neatly made as they sing :

> When you wake up in the morning,
>   At the day dawning,
> Throw off the bedding and let it all air,
>   Then shake up the pillows,
>   In waves and in billows,
> And leave them near windows, if the day is quite fair.

Linen, clean and white, is such a delight, we shall all be interested in the washing lesson. Tiny tubs and shining little washboards; fresh clothes-lines hung from posts set in the four corners of the rooms; baby clothes-pins, and a bag of soiled doll-sized garments—this is the equipment. The clothes are sorted, then washed, the girls singing:

> In the tub so cheerily,
> Our little hands must go,
> Washing all so merrily,
> And washing white as snow.
>
> While we wash, oh, readily,
> So white the garments grow,
> Rub and scrub them steadily,
> And let clear water flow.

Everything pertaining to laundry work is taught, boiling, rinsing and bluing, hanging the clothes on the line, followed by instruction as to sprinkling, folding and ironing.

The sweeping lesson is one of the liveliest, and includes dusting, how to wipe the woodwork, and putting the room in order as they sing:

> Away now, swiftly flying,
> It is our sweeping day;
> For brooms and dusters plying
> To work without delay;
> First open shutters wide,
> Move little things outside.
>
> CHORUS—Then sweep, sweep, sweep, my little maid,
> To make your room so neat.

Scrubbing is hardly an æsthetic or specially delightful exercise, and yet one might almost believe it were both, watching that little company of workers with their scrubbing brushes, three inches long, polishing the table in front of them, as they merrily sing:

> Scrubbing away
> At break of day,
> To make our homes look neatly;
> For a good hard scrub is the very best way,
> To make all smell so sweetly.

CHORUS—Then scrub away in your very best way,
    With face so bright and cheerful ;
    For a cheery face meets much more grace
    Then one that's always tearful.

The lessons taught include making fires, handling matches, and taking care of ashes and coal, waiting on the door and table, setting and clearing off the latter. A " pricking lesson" teaches the parts of beef and mutton, and how to cut and cook each.

WHAT JAMIE SAID TO THE MOON.

L AST night the moon rose from the deep blue lake,
It saw a city full of children take
Sweet rest in quiet sleep from God the Giver;
It watched all night, lake, city, people, river.

    *   *   *   *   *   *   *   *

"My mamma said the moon looked pale and sad.
Maybe it wondered if we children had
Each prayed our prayer before we came to bed,
And thanked the Lord for all the Saviour said.

"What did you think, poor moon, as on you sailed,
Away up there, alone, and never failed
To go just on the errands you were sent?
I wish *we* always did just what we meant.

"You never stop to play behind a cloud;
If you *should* run away, or *should* speak loud,
Cross angry words up there, with heav'n so near,
The stars would be afraid, and God would hear!

"Are you the mamma of the stars? tell me,
I wonder at most everything I see—
I'll never tell the secret, if I only knew.
I think our world is beautiful, don't you?

"Good moon, you've taught me—Oh, so many things!
I *love* you, moon; if I only had wings,
I'd fly to see you in your blue sky-sea.
I think 'twould be so nice, just you and me."

HOW TO TEACH READING.

BY ANTONIA ROESER, NEWARK, N. J.

 begin with a lesson on the chart, and illustrate it by making pictures on the blackbord. I then allow my class to think for a moment, and if ready, hands will be up to tell me all they can about the pictures or objects. I then write the pupils sentences on the blackboard, and ask questions frequently ; I also allow questions by the pupils, as I find it gives them thinking power.

When I have written these sentences, we learn all the words and pronounce them beginning at the top and then at the bottom, skipping all over, and rub out words occasionally, to keep the attention of scholars as well as to see how quickly they can read. The class is interested, and by letting children do the talking, they lose all diffidence, as well as gain confidence in their teachers.

When a lesson is very hard and I see children lose interest, I put a new one on the black-board, but return to the old one in a few days, with a different picture, using the same words with a few new ones, and I find the children as much interested as if it were entirely new.

For variety I hold up objects, make pictures of them on the blackboard, and they tell me all they can about them. I then write these sentences on the blackboard, and let my class read them as well as they can. For review I will put a picture of some previous lesson on the blackboard and see how many can remember all about that lesson. I then let them write it, and read every word they write. I have no

difficulty in teaching new words, as I notice children compare forms and sounds of words. When I put a new word
on the blackboard, I let my class first pronounce it slowly,
then I give the sounds, then let some pupil give the sepa-
rate sounds, and lastly, I spell it. I have sentences written
on cardboard, which I distribute to the class to see how
readily they can read them. Some are questions, others
are answers. Those who have questions, I allow to make
answers, and *vice versa.* Then I have other slips with the
words *is, are am, an, etc., etc.,* on them ; the pupils take
these and make sentences, using the words properly. I have
also pasted pictures on bristol board, with the names of the
pictures, and pupils tell all they can about them, and also
write about them, and then read it in the class. Sometimes
I let them think of all the words they have had during the
week. They pronounce, sound, and read every word they
write. They seem to enjoy thinking for themselves very
much.

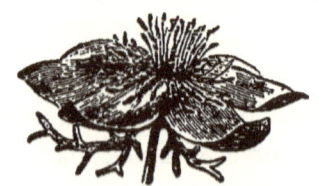

DEPTHS AND HEIGHTS.

OUT of the depths I cry;
　　I have no speech beside;
And clouds and tempests nigh
　　Conceal the Crucified.

Mine eyes are dim of sight;
　　I can not trace the way;
The darkness is as night,
　　And night without a day.

Mine hands hang helpless down;
　　Life's burden presses sore;
Alike seems cross and crown—
　　The Now and Evermore.

Nor can the weary feet
　　Press onward in the race,
Unless, in Whom complete,
　　The heart find needed grace.

Out of the depths I cry;
　　I have no speech beside;
Lord, from thy throne on high,
　　Reveal the Crucified.

Upon the crowning heights I stand,
　　A victor strong and free;
And hope illumines all the land,
　　And heart holds jubilee.

No more do clouds and tempests hide
  The father's smiling face ;
Beside me walks the Crucified,
  In form of sweetest grace. .

Around, above, a glory shines ;
  Bright day supplants the night ;
And all my sorrow he refines,
  And makes each burden light.

He hears my prayer, and grants His care.
  In loving providence ;
With art most rare, when harm would snare,
  He shields from consequence.

No more distrust, no more despair ,
  The waters can not whelm ;
The bark sails safe through foul and fair—
  His hand is on the helm.

FUN WITH A SPIDER.

SPIDERS in many respects are just like other animals and can be tamed and petted, and taught a great many lessons which they will learn as readily as a dog or cat. But you must take the trouble to study their ways and get on the good side of them.

One day I had been reading a book how spiders managed to get their webs across streams and roads, and from the top of one tall tree to another. I went out and caught a large garden spider, one of those blue-gray sprawling fellows, and fixed him for my experiment.

I took a stick about eighteen inches in length, and fastened a piece of iron to one end of it, so that the stick would stand up on that end of itself. Then I put this stick in the center of a large tub of water, and placed the spider on top of the stick. I wanted to see if he could get to the "land," which was the edge of the tub, without any help. He ran down first one side of the stick, and then the other; each time he would stop when he touched the water, and shaking his foot as a cat does, he would run up again. At last he came to the conclusion that he was entirely surrounded by water— on an island, in fact. After remaining perfectly quiet for a long while, during which I have no doubt he was arranging his plans, he began running around the top of the stick, and throwing out great coils of web, with his hind feet. In a few minutes little fine strings of web were floating away in the slight breeze that was blowing. After a little one of these threads touched the edge of the tub, and stuck fast, as all spider webs will do.

This was just what Mr. Spider was looking for, and the next minute he took hold of his web, and gave it a jerk, as a sailor does with a rope when he wishes to see how strong it is or make it fast.   Having satisfied himself that it was fast at the other end, he gathered it in till it was tight and straight, and then ran on it quickly to the shore; a rescued castaway saved by his own ingenuity.

Spiders are not fools, if they are ugly, and He who made all things has a thought, and care for all.   The earth is full of the knowledge of God.

THANKSGIVING.

BY SYLVIA BROWN.

ING, heart of mine, the year is young,
  The buds are bursting on the trees,
The swelling hopes of life are thine
  And float in song on every breeze.

Sing, heart of mine, the summer bloom;
  Its fragrant perfume fills the air;
Now life is rich, for Love and Faith
  Within the soul their incense bear.

Sing, heart of mine, the year is ripe.
  Full harvests bless the fruitful land;
Life's royal fruitage waiteth, too,
  The tender Master's garnering hand.

Sing, heart of mine, the year is done,
  Chill winter spreads her silver vest,
Life's fruit is with its gathered sheaves,
  Thy year is done, now wait thy rest.

Sing, heart of mine, for God is just
  Who gives the waiting earth his care:
The spring-time, rain, the bud and bloom,
  The cooling dew to summer air.

Sing, heart of mine, for God is good
  Who fills the ear and bending sheaf;
Who hides the clusters of the vine
  Beneath the golden autumn leaf.

Sing, heart of mine! Oh, praise his name,
  Whose loving care hath blessed our store;
With glad thanksgiving praise his name
  Whose care surrounds us evermore.

The Rules of Good Health,

AND

HOW TO PROMOTE IT.

I give my opinion on the Rules of Good Health, and how I think Children should be raised to be moral and healthy.

THE great question may be asked throughout the world, as to what is health, and we most willingly answer by saying, that good health is that condition of the body and mind, which enables both to per_ fo:m their duties properly, and without pain. Some one part of the body, such as a finger, or limb, can become disabled or in other words taken from the body, without any injury to general health. For after the wounded part of the body becomes healed up, such persons will enjoy their physical health as much as any other living person. And if you will notice you will see that our health is in our own keeping, or, in other words, to a great extent it depends on ourselves, whether life bodily, and mentally is happy, or whether it turns out a wretched failure. So I urge upon the reader, that there is a gospel for the body, and for the mind of man, as well as for the moral department, of his nature. The same God made all these, and cares for them all, as Christ proved by connecting bodily and mental cares with the salvation of the soul; as the whole man belongs to God, we are bound to take care of every part. If any one ask, why can't I do as I like, the answer is found in the fact, that we are stewards under God; health tends to make us all happy, and it is God's wish that we should be happy.

13

We have no right to bring a moment's unhappiness, on our-selves, by transgression against, or by neglect of his laws.

Every living person should learn themselves, to retire at the proper hour for bedtime, so as to rise early next morn-ing, and walk out and inhale the pure fresh morning air. Some people expose themselves to a great extent, by too much hard labor, some will work both day and night, and in all kinds of bad weather, in order to make, and save money, and gain wealth, which is very good, but re-member that it is just as important, and more so, to labor and manage to save your health ; for after you are dead, what good will the money do you. Hard daily laboring people should learn themselves to retire to their beds of rest at nine o'clock, or not later than half past, so that they may have plenty of time to sleep and rest. We should eat our meals regular, and those of good, well cooked wholesome food, and light meals for supper. It is good for us to exercise our muscles all we can, either by labor, walking or moving in some form ; and let us lay aside the use of our strong tobacco, for about two months trial, and at the expiration of that time, when we find ourselves feeling so much better, and stronger, looking better in the face, and a lot of money saved, we will be so rejoiced, that we will never want to taste tobacco again. Let every man turn his back on strong drink the same way. Use pure soft filtered rain water for external as well as internal use.

KEEP YOUR ROOMS VENTILATED.

It matters not how cold the winter days may be. Give your house ventilation, especially your bed rooms where you sleep with the rooms all closed up so close, that the foul air accumulated over night has no way of escape, which we think would not be pleasant for good health. Leave a small ventilation to your bed room, both day and night, either from the transom or window, so the pure, dry air can pass in the room, and the foul air as it accumulates over night, can pass out. And first when you rise every morning, open your windows, and dust out, and give ventilation to your bed rooms all day, until just after sunset. Leave your window open so the sun may shine in your bed rooms some part of the day. Remember that corn, wheat, and plants of all kinds must have air, and the heat of the sun, or they can not grow, healthy. And just so it is with man. He must have fresh air, and feel the heat of the sun, which must shine upon him at times, or he can not live and enjoy good health.

TO RAISE CHILDREN TO BE MORAL AND HEALTHY.

To raise young children to be moral and healthy is not to feed them on too strong food while in their youth. Never allow them to drink tea or coffee. Forbid your children making use of strong drinks of any kind. Tea and coffee are too stimulating for their nervous system ; it is weakening to their constitution. Forbid them putting any drinks in their mouths, stronger than cold water, and sweet milk, which is made for children, all they can drink; and after they pass the age of twelve, and thirteen years, without using strong drinks at the table, both the child and its parents will see how much better off, and how much better they look, by not being allowed to use strong drink. Such children will ever refrain from the habits of strong drink as long as they live—such as tea, coffee, and rum. The best way to raise little children to be good, to love their parents, and to be polite and mannerly, is to train them up by kind words, and to avoid whipping them as much as possible.

Forbid them keeping late hours at night.   Put them early
to bed, in order that they may get from ten to eleven hours
sleep ; the more sleep they get, the faster and stronger they
will grow, but you must commence with them in time.   My
opinion is, that young children will learn faster, think quicker,
and grow much healthier, by not having their feet bound up
in real tight shoes ; much better that they go barefooted in
the summer season of the year, and when they do wear
shoes, let them be loose on their feet, on account of the cir-
culation of the blood from the feet to the brain ; and another thought is that it might be well for a child in every
sense, that the best moral influence surrounds its early
youth.   By the time a child reaches five or seven years of
age, it ought to have a great deal of education — both boys
and girls.   They should have some well fixed ideas about
right and wrong in its own condition.   It should first be
taught to know that it is subject to authority, and it should
also appreciate that the authority is justice, tempered with
mercy.   Moral and religious ideas may be impressed upon
young minds before lessons, from books by letters and
figures.

SLEEP AND REST.

Laboring people who exercise themselves at hard daily
labor, should have their rest at night.   Such persons should
retire to bed, in time to get as much as eight hours sleep ;
students eight and a half; children ten and eleven hours.
And if you find it difficult to get to sleep, you should remain
in bed next morning, a short time at entire rest ; or you
should retire to rest sooner at night, in order to make up the
lost sleep.   Plenty of good sleep is a great addition to health,
it helps to throw off disease.   You should take a short nap
every day in the summer season, just after eating your din-

ner, remaining about twenty-five minutes asleep, if time will admit.

Some laboring people will work hard all day, and then stay up half the night, plundering around, losing sleep and breaking their rest, which is injurious to any one's health. God has provided sleep and rest for ever person, which they should make use of at the proper time.

KEEP YOUR FEET WARM AND DRY.

To avoid colds and rheumatism, keep your feet warm and dry. Never take off your shoes to warm your feet, or to cool them. If you do you are bound to take cold. We find it to be a common rule for a great many women, and some men, who make a habit after working hard all day, to slip off their shoes to rest their feet at night, while setting around before going to bed, and also to cool or to warm them. Such exposure leaves persons subject to rheumatism, which we know to be very hard to get rid of. They will remain for hours with their shoes off, until their feet get cold. Never take your shoes from your feet until you are ready for bed. The best remedy for colds and sick headache, is to bath your feet in luke warm salt water, and drink all the cold water you can on going to bed.

FORBID YOUNG BOYS THE USE OF TOBACCO.

The use of tobacco is a habit, that should be done away with among the young; they should especially avoid the habit. It gives a doubtful pleasure for a certain penalty. Accumulated facts go to show, that growing boys are the worse mentally, and physically, for the use of tobacco. It should be kept out of the schools as far as possible. It is injurious to growing boys, especially schools boys, as it destroys the nervous system, and makes the boy stubborn, unconcerned, disobedient, idle, and reckless and unfits him for study. Remember that over two-thirds of the young boys, that are raised under the influence of strong tobacco, will become lovers of strong drinks, which will lead them to be drunkards. And if they do not reform from the evil habit, it will, in time, destroy both soul, and body forever. There is a duty involved upon both school teacher, and the parents of children, to see after the school boys, and forbid them using tobacco in any form. My advice to young men is to refrain from the use of tobacco ; for the use of it weakens and destroys the nervous system to a great extent, and more than that it is a bad habit. A person should never put anything in their mouth that they have to spit from. As soon as you put tobacco in your mouth, the effect produced on the saliva causes the gastric juice to flow, until a large quantity has escaped, or as long as the action in the mouth continues. So the person who uses tobacco throws away just what nature demands we should retain with us, which helps to keep the body in a healthy state.

ALCOHOL.

Remember that alcohol is capable of damaging each and every organ and tissue of the human body. There is always danger in the path of him, whose appetite, and passions have been, not his servants, but his masters. Hence, alcohol becomes a dangerous instrument even in the hands of the strong, and the wise ; a murderous instrument in the hands of the foolish, and weak. If used too excessively, the monster evil, will degrade the character of both men and women, and lead them from degredation to an untimely grave. Scientific physicians, the world over, have been engaged for years, in the investigation of the subject, and the universal verdict is, that the use of alcohol is productive of a vast deal of harm. In a lecture on this subject an article, delivered by Dr. Norman Kerr, of England, says: "that diseases might be broadly divided, into those that were, and those that were not preventable ; those arising from needless personal habits, were the more numerous and important, and their consideration was concentrated, on one great group of preventive diseases." It was admitted that intoxicating drinks were not essential to the healthy, they were luxuries, not necessities ; hence they could safely be dispensed with ; so all diseases springing from the limited or unlimited use of intoxicants were preventable diseases.

THE EVIL OF INTEMPERANCE.

Above all things withdraw yourselves from the use of intoxicating liquors, as a beverage, as it is injurious to the welfare, health, and morals of the people, and also a stumbling block to the church of God. Take notice that if a man never takes the first drink of whiskey, he will never become a drunkard. Let whiskey, ale, beer and wine stay to itself, and you will never have to suffer from the effects of intoxicating liquors. The injury that alcohol inflicts on the human system, has been set forth by the most competent investigators, that the worst effect is on the brain. Alcohol is no where to be found in any product of nature ; it was never itself " created by the living God." . It is nothing more than an artificial concern prepared by the skill of man, through the desrtuctive process prepared, for the purpose of a speculation, and to be used in some respects as a medicine, by applying so much alcohol to some other remedy. But it goes on to show that perfect health can only be obtained, by total abstinence from all intoxicating drinks ; as they only drain the natural functions of the body. There

are numbers of persons who suffer and die from different dis·
eases, which are brought upon themselves, by the use of
strong drinks.

THEY STAYED ON THE FARM.

FOR WHICH I THANK ISADORE ROGERS.

I was tired that night, and it did seem as if there was everything to discourage, and nothing to cheer. Will, our oldest boy, had come from his work with a discontented look upon his countenance, saying, that he wished he was in his consin Harold's place, with nothing to do but stand behind a counter, and measure goods all day, having everything he wanted, and no work worth mentioning. And when Jenny asked for a new white dress, there was nothing that I would have enjoyed so much as to have been able to give it to her, for I like to see my children nicely dressed, as my mother. But when I told her that we could not afford it, she did not realize that it was as much of a privation to me as to her, and said :

" Well mother, if you can not afford it, I can do nicely without it," after the manner of dutiful daughters in stories ; but she went away looking as if nothing but my selfishness withheld it from her.

You can never realize the situation unless I tell you exactly how it is, and I don't want you to understand that I am saying a word against John, for he has more real good and manly traits than any other man of my acquaintance ; but he is so easy and good-natured that he would hand out the last dollar in the world to indulge the children, if I said so, when he knew that he had a note for farming implements coming due that very day.

I knew exactly how much money he had—just enough to pay the interest on the mortgage, and not a dollar more ; and it was only by the strictest economy in household expenditures that he had that, for I had bought all the grocer-

ies and *necessary* clothing for the children, by the sale of but-
ter and eggs.   Beside, his note for the new reaper would be
coming due before lòng, and with his improvident ways, I
knew that if I didn't keep a sharp look out there would be no
money for that.   We were what was considered a well-to-do
farmer's family.   Our credit was good anywhere, but mercy
knows how much care and management it took to keep it so.

When the children asked him for anything, he always answered, "Just as your mother says ;" and with all the care
and responsibility of looking ahead thrown upon me, I was
obliged to say no so often, they began to look upon me as
being the cause of all their denials, when heaven knows that
I was only trying to secure a home that was our very own,
where they might enjoy comfort and plenty in their youthful days, and return on Christmas and Thanksgiving as long
as they lived.

And for this object I had toiled, economized, and denied
myself in every possible way ; and although I could see that
with the slow but steady progress that we were making, the
grand object would be accomplished in a few years more,
the fact that I received credit for nothing, but having a constant desire to economize, from my children, and a disposition to fret about nothing (as he called it, when I tried to
impress upon him the importance of being prepared to meet
his payments), from my husband, made my lot seem doubly
hard to bear.

Jennie was fifteen years old — just the age to like pretty
dresses with flowers and ribbons, without realizing that they
do not grow upon bushes, from which the paternal hands
have but to reach forth and take them ; and just after she
went away, with discontent written upon her features, John
came in.

"Susan," said he, complainingly, "I do wish you would
discard that habit of fretting about matters that will come

out all right anyway. Such a countenance is enough to give a man a fit of the blues."

Now, I am very well aware that matters never came right unless there was a power at work to bring them right; and as for a fit of despondency, I knew that he was never troubled with any such malady. And for a moment, I felt as if I would rather he should be grasping and stingy, than to be so utterly reckless and improvident, that he could not even sympathize with my care and anxiety. Right here let me say, wives do not blame your husbands too severely for what appears to you like mere avariciousness, when there is a mortgage on the farm, and other expenses to meet of which you do not have the care and responsibility.

I felt so discouraged, so much in need of some one to understand and smypathize with my motives, that I was in no mood to reply, and beside I knew that it would be of no use, anyway, so I went out into the yard and left him alone.

"I won't try any more," I said, petulantly. "One may wear her life away for husband and children, and instead of receiving credit for the one hundred things that she does for their comfort, she will be censured for one that they deem amiss."

But a woman with five children to fit for useful and honorable lives, has a burden upon her shoulders which she cannot lay down whenever she feels that her efforts are unappreciated. But she must be content to wait patiently until the ripening years bring their reward, no matter how long and weary it may seem. All this dawned upon me as I walked alone under the shade trees that grew about our dwelling, and as earnest reflection succeeded the transient outburst of impatience and discouragement, I set about devising some remedy for the evils which I could not ignore.

At length, refreshed by my walk, and recovered from my petulant mood, I returned to the house. Jennie was looking over her last year's lawns and ribbons, with rather a dejected expression of countenance, and I really felt sorry for her as I noticed how shabby they were.

"Jennie," said I, "I am sorry that I cannot give you the dress, but perhaps we can find some way for you to get it yourself."

"Do you mean that I may go out to work, and earn money with which to buy it?" she asked, wonderingly.

"No, I answered; "you are growing, yet, and people who employ help will not spare you, as your mother does, by doing all the heaviest work themselves, that your young shoulders may grow straight and strong, without being dwarfed and disfigured by tasks too great for a growing girl ; and beside, I think that there should be work on the farm, for all the members of a family."

"There has always been work enough, mercy knows," said Jennie, dolefully.

"But I have been trying to think of some way in which you can earn money for your own expenses, and if you get it and expend it yourself, you will realize that you have it more than when you have nothing, excepting what we buy and bring to you. Suppose that you take the row of currant bushes on the east side of the garden for your own, gather and sell the fruit yourself, and buy the dress, or anything else that you want.

"Can I really have all the money that the currants will bring?" she asked, brightening up, and putting away the faded dress and ribbons.

"Yes," I replied, "and you will need even more next year, than this. It is only by looking ahead, and preparing for the future, that we may have plenty for the present; and if you will plant a large bed of strawberries. and cultivate them yourself, you can have all they will yield.

"May I have a bed, too?" asked Alice, my thirteen-year-

old girl, who had entered the room, and stood listening to
the conversation.

" Yes, if you will cultivate it yourself, and keep your
plants free from weeds," I answered.

" And do just what I please, with the money ? " she ques-
tioned.

" Yes, but I shall require you to make your purchases
carefully, that you may receive the full value of your money,"
I replied.

"Oh, you can go with me, and assist with your advice,"
she answered, " if I can only have the money, and buy the
dresses and other things myself."

" What can *I* have, mamma ? " asked Nellie, who had
reached the age of six years.

" I will give you two nice Brahma hens, and you may
have all the little chicks, if you feed and take care of them
yourself."

"We shall soon be as well off as the boys, for all Will feels
so proud of his pigs, and George of his turkeys," and the
child ran off, gleefully, to look up a good location for a
couple of hen coops. The older girls went speedily to work
at their strawberry beds, and before another day had passed
each had a nicely prepared piece of ground, with two hundred plants.

And Jennie manifested a new interest in those currant
bushes, which had been somewhat neglected for a year or
two past. She dug away the grass, and carried pailfuls of
dirt from the chip-yard to put around the roots, for she said
if *she* were going to raise fruit for the market, it should be
of the very best quality, and the improvement was really
surprising.

What a new interest the girls seemed to take in everything ! They did their work in the house with unusual
alacrity, that they might have a few moments to work with

their plants before school time, and not a weed was allowed to grow to the detriment of their enterprise. Jennie realized a greater sum than I had anticipated from the sale of the currants. The dress was purchased, and several articles besides, but it was not until the following year that the real profit began.

The girls had procured a treatise upon the culture of small fruits, and attended to the plants according to directions, and all their care and labor was amply rewarded by the large yield and fine quality of their berries. They had money, without being obliged even to ask for it, with which to purchase new school books, as well as new hats, ribbons, and dresses, beside supplying our own table with delicious fruit all through the season.

"Mother," said Jennie, after the last of the berries had been gathered, "strawberries last but a short time ; would it not be well to have a quantity of raspberry plants set out, that we may gather from them when the strawberries are gone ? "

"It would be a good plan, certainly," I answered.

" And I'll plant blackberries to follow the raspberries," said Will.

" And I'll raise grapes to come after the blackberries," said George.

" I have lots of chickens," said little Nellie, with such a look of importance that her brothers smiled.

And each went to work to have something from which to supply his own private purse.

The berries took but little more time and attention than the same amount of corn or potatoes, but the boys could not be spared from the field to pick berries, so they gave the girls a share to gather and market them, observing that they could keep even, anyway, since they had other means which the girls had not. And with money with which to gratify so many of their desires, each subscribed for a periodical adapted to his individual taste. Will took a good agricultural paper, George another from a different part of the country, Jennie and Alice each a magazine, and Nellie sold her chickens, bought a new cloak, and subscribed for a child's paper.

The fact of individual ownership gives all these an added value, and this class of reading is rapidly leading their youthful minds toward progress and intelligence. They are happy and contented, without the least desire to leave the farm, where there is profitable employment for all, and a recognition of the right of each to control at least a share of his own earnings, instead of being compelled to work in the ceaseless treadmill of the general welfare, with only the individuality of the father recognized, as is too apt to be the case where the boys are discontented and anxious to leave the farm.

And instead of being a tax upon our resources, the children are self-supporting, and proud of the independence which their industry gives them, and never were girls more rosy and healthy than ours. Their is no longer any necessity for that grinding economy which we were once obliged to practice, and John sometimes says:

"Don't you see, Susan, that our affairs are coming out all right, even though I never worried and fretted about it?"

WHEAT AND FIELD FLOWERS.

BY MRS. J. B. WILCOX.

"AS a lilly among thorns, so is my love among the daughters." And my love is a book, a rare new book, which meets every want of my heart. Though it does not, like another book lately published, bear the title, "Ein Wort," the one word, "Liebe," is its soul and inspiration. This book is my good companion all the day long. It mourns with me when I am sad. It rejoices with me when I am glad. It reproves my faults. It inspires me to good deeds. And like all our very dearest loves, it is choice, and reserves its gifts for a few.

When in mournful mood I turn to my book, I find words so tender and tearful they seem to be but the echoes of my own sad heart set to sweet music, and in them, I breathe out my complaint:

> To you the day is fair,
> As days may be,
> My eyes are filled too bitterly with tears
> To see.
> You view a thousand graves
> And sigh at none,
> My heart is breaking at the simple thought
> Of one.

Or sympathy comes to one in such words as these:

> There are, who for thy last, long sleep,
> Shall sleep as sweetly, nevermore,
> Shall weep because thou canst not weep,
> And grieve because thy griefs are o'er.
>
> Sad thrift of love! the loving breast
> On which thy aching head is thrown,
> Will give the weary head to rest,
> But keep the aching for its own.

When I am glad, I find songs like joy-bells to express my gladness :

> A smile into my heart has crept,
>   And laughs through all my being,
> New joy into my life has leapt,
>   The joy of only seeing !
>
> O happy glow, O sun-bathed tree,
>   O golden lighted river,
> A love-gift has been given to me,
> And which of you is giver?

The words of reproof from my book, my love, seem too personal and sacred to be shared with others, but there are inspirations that it would be ungenerous to keep to one's self :

> There are poems unwritten and songs unsung
>   Sweeter than any that ever were heard,
> Poems that wait for an angel tongue ;
>   Songs that but long for a Paradise bird,
> Poems that ripple through lowliest lives,
>   Poems unnoted and hidden away,
> Down in the souls where the beautiful thrives,
>   Sweetly as flowers in the air of the May—
> Poems, that only the angels above us,
>   Looking down deep in our hearts, may behold ;
> Felt though unseen, by the beings that love us,
>   Written on lives as of in letters of gold,
> Sing to my soul the sweet song that thou livest,
>   Read me the poem that never was penned.
> The wonderful idyl of life that thou givest
>   Fresh from thy spirit, O beautiful friend.

And my treasure, my book, is rare :

> It hoards not, yet it rests content,
> And not unsought will give.

For it is published for only a few friends, to whom it is presented by the editor and compiler. It is the tribute of one choice, sweet soul to another, whose beautiful and saintly life seems to color every page. We have among our Christmas books, "Fifty Perfect Poems," but this is, through all its lines, "one grand sweet song." In the following inspiring words lies the secret of the two lives that are woven into it :

The spirit which from God is made,
  The noblest of its kind
Asks not the help of rules that serve,
  To guide the feeble mind.
It soars, however bold its flight,
  Right onward, safe and free,
And all that schools and books can teach,
  In its own self can see
What charms this soul all souls must charm ;
  What grieves it saddens all ;
It holds the choicest of the world
  Within its subtle thrall.

The book is copyrighted by Mrs. Alice L. Williams, a
name that is to many who have shared in the overflowing
bounties of her sunny nature, as that of a fairy queen, who
can bring the most impossible things to pass.   The next
page reads : " Dedicated to my friend, Lucy Perry Noble,
who is God's best gift to so many loving hearts."   And
throughout its four-hundred and thirty-four pages, we
breathe the spirit of these two elect women.   The editor
speaks to us mostly through choice selections, but sometimes, we are sure, in her own words, modestly veiled under
the signature, " Anon," or " From the German."   These
are some of the more direct tributes to her friend.

TO L. P. N.

I asked the Sun,
Canst thou tell me what love is ?
He answered only a smile
    Of golden light.

I prayed the flowers,
Oh, tell me what is love ?
Only a fragrant sigh was wafted
    Through the night.

Is love the soul's true life?
Or is but the sport
Of idle summer hours ?   I asked
    Of Heaven above.

In answer, God sent thee,
Dear heart, to me ;
And I no longer question,
    What is love.

And again

My peace thou art,
My firm, green isle without a troubled sea,
And lying here and looking upward now, ?
I ask, if thou art this, what God must be?
If thus I rest within *thy* goodness, how
In goodness of the infinite degree?

It is impossible in this limited space to do justice to this book. Its "Tributes to Wives and Mothers," its "Handful of Letters," and its "Service of Sorrow," with sweet words "In Memoriam" that recall the very presence of loved ones of whom we say,

The waiting angels bade them
Go up higher,

make it a store house of treasures for many hearts. And those who have long felt, that the dear friend to whom it is dedicated walked among us an uncrowned queen, give thanks and blessings to her who has woven this chaplet of laurels for her brow. It is a beautiful thing when, as in the "In Memoriam" of Tennyson, the loving tribute of a friend gives a new life to one who has passed into the Silent Land. It is a more beautiful thing when the "best gift of God, immortal love," finds expression in singing the praises of a living friend, and iliumines her life with a radiance that can not be hidden from the eyes of others, making it a joy, and an inspiration to many who are tempted to believe that life is not worth living.

The wish has been very widely expressed that another edition of "Wheat and Field Flowers" might be published for general sale, and we feel confident that such a universal wish will not be disappointed.

A WORKER'S SONG.

IT is not for me to order,
   The work that I have to do;
My eyes must follow the Master,
   And ever His will pursue.
And therefore I wait and listen,
   For as soon as I hear His voice,
Forward I press with gladness,
   And even in toil rejoice.

Sometimes I can hear Him calling,
   To tasks that are great and high;
I should often fear to attempt them,
   But that He is standing by;
Sometimes unto service lowly,
   That even a child might do,
Comes the Master's kindly summons,
   And hearing I hasten through.

Oh! none can be sad or gloomy
   In the hours they work for Him,
For He smileth aye upon us,
   Let the day be bright or dim.
And we cheer our hearts with singing,
   While busy at our tasks;
It is but faithful service
   That the gracious Master asks.

Sometimes I am growing weary,
   And by troublous cares opprest,
And the Master, in His pity,
   Dismisses me to rest.

And, again, when I have not earned it,
  In His kindly, great regard,
He loads me, not with wages,
  But munificent reward.

Oh! who that once has served Him
  Will any other serve?
Oh! who that ever has seen Him
  Will from His fealty swerve.
Come all, and be His servants,
  For He your friend will be,
All gracious and forgiving, still,
  As He has been to me.

ONE of the highest duties of a missionary is, to first work to spread the gospel of Christ throughout the land, that it may be preached unto every living creature. Foreign mission work is conducted by giving and soliciting funds, to send ministers and other teachers, as missionaries, with Bibles to the foreign countries, that they may preach and teach the gospel of Christ to the different nations, such as Africa, Asia, China, and India, that they may be brought from darkness unto the light of Christian civilization. The missionary shall also give and solicit funds to send to the above named countries for the purpose of erecting church buildings for public worship and organizing Sabbath-schools. The home work for the missionary is to work in aid of the gospel of Christ being preached to the poor throughout the United States of America. To make their home work a success, they should first unite themselves together in clubs, and organize in the different churches, what should be known as the Womens' Home and Foreign Missionary Society. But such societies can be organized independent, without regard to church, creed, or denomination, and each member of said society is duty bound to pay her initiation fee on entering as full members, and also to pay weekly or monthly dues, to the amount of whatever may be required by the constitution of the society, and it is also the duty of each individual member to solicit funds from the public, for the purpose of helping to build a missionary treasury, and all funds of said treasury are to be contributed to aid the destitute, sick, and afflicted persons who are actually known to be unable to help themselves, those persons residing in the same county, city, or village, where said missionary society may be located. The above named persons we consider the home circle sufferers, who are entitled to receive the first benefits of said society; after which, it shall be the duty of the society to draw money from the same treasury, which shall be contributed to the aid of the destitute and needy anywhere throughout the United States, wherever appeals are made for help, and the society feels itself able to respond, which will be to send donations, such as money or clothing, to relieve the destitute and suffering of our country. The societies will also purchase books, Bibles, and testaments, to aid and assist poor Sabbath-schools, and to organize new ones wherever they are needed in all parts of this country, and to assist traveling missionaries in going forth proclaiming the gospel of Christ to the poor. They will cheerfully contribute to aid in building up disabled churches, when applications are made to them for help.

SABBATH-SCHOOLS.

The missionary societies that are organized in the different Sabbath-schools, are for the purpose of raising funds to be expended for the support of both the home and foreign missionary cause. It is the duty of all teachers and scholars of the various Sabbath-schools to canvass their own city, village or neighborhood, where such schools are located, and bring in the children from the highways and hedges who never attend any school and are violating the Sabbath from time to time, and are growing up in their sins without ever being taught to know there is a God whom they must serve. Teachers and scholars who go out as missionaries and find these poor, forgotten children, should, before removing them, first go and consult their parents or guardians, if they have such, and after receiving their consent, the canvasser should oblige such children to attend some good Sabbath-school, by bringing them forward and making them welcome in the several classes, that these children may learn the lessons which tell them what God will have them to do, that they may become fol-. lowers of Christ our Lord.

THE CLOSING SUBJECT.

In conclusion, I take great pleasure to inform the public at large, that for the sake of suffering humanity, I hereby resolve to donate to the missionary cause, from two and a half to five cents out of every dollar that I may realize from the sale of my book, which shall be deposited in the treasury, to be used for the relief of the destitute and suffering people of our county, at home and abroad. These donations will be made according as I prosper in making sales of the book.

Yours,   SAM'L EASON.